THE LOVERS' GRAVES

D1514327

THE LOVERS' GRAVES

Six True Tales that Shocked Wales

Bethan Phillips

gomer

First published in 2007 by
Gomer Press, Llandysul, Ceredigion, SA44 4JL

Second impression 2007

ISBN 978 1 84323 790 7

A CIP record for this title is available from the British Library.

© Copyright: Bethan Phillips, 2007

Bethan Phillips asserts her moral right under the
Copyright, Designs and Patents Act, 1988
to be identified as author of this work.

All rights reserved. No part of this book may be reproduced,
stored in a retrieval system, or transmitted in any form
or by any means, electronic, electrostatic, magnetic tape, mechanical,
photocopying, recording or otherwise without permission
in writing from the above publishers.

This book is published with the financial support of the
Welsh Books Council.

Printed and bound in Wales at
Gomer Press, Llandysul, CeredigionSecon

To my mother Phyllis Richards (née Trevena),
born in South Africa. Although she died young,
her influence upon me never waned.

Acknowledgements

I received a great deal of willing assistance from many people in preparing this book. I relied heavily on the recollections of those who shared their memories with me and who provided me with many of the photographs. I am particularly grateful to Thomas Lloyd O.B.E. for his encouragement and sound advice. Others who readily provided me with information were Evan and Bet Davis of Oak Hill, Ohio, the late Reverend Peter Braby, Vicar of Badsey, and the late Elisabeth Inglis Jones, whose letters over the years proved to be invaluable sources. I relied heavily on the staff of a number of institutions, and would mention the National Library of Wales, Cheetham's Library, Manchester, Ceredigion Library and the Ceredigion Museum. I'm also indebted to Mr Herbert Hughes of Brecon and Mr Gerald Morgan.

Lampeter Town Council unearthed the photograph of William Jones, and Michael Freeman kindly produced a copy of it. Many local people have shown an interest in these stories and responded to my innumerable questions. Unfortunately, some are no longer with us, and these include Mrs Jano Griffiths, Mrs Nancy Williams, Mrs Bell, Mr Gwyn Evans J.P., Mr Tommy Williams and Mr Dafydd Jones. Others who gave of their time are Mrs Beti Davies, who first drew the graves to my attention, and her husband John Davies, Mr Rhuthwyn Jones, Mr Ieuan Williams and Mr Tommy Thomas. Photographs were provided by Mrs Gwyneth Jones, Mrs Iris Quan and Miss Myra Pugh. Mr Eric Formby of Battle, a descendant of Edward Hesketh Formby, went to the trouble of sending me many documents relating to his uncle's estate. I am particularly indebted to Mr Tim Jones, photographer, Lampeter, and to Mr Robert Blayney for their contributions. I would also like to express my gratitude to the late Mr Julian Cayo Evans who gave me access to Glandenys and to Dalis and Rhodri who continued to welcome me into the mansion.

Finally, my thanks go to Ceri Wyn Jones of Gomer Press, who took the book through the onerous process of publication. Any outstanding defects are entirely mine.

Contents

The Lovers' Graves – today neglected and ravaged by time. *pic. Tim Jones*

Preface

The story of the two graves situated on a lonely spot overlooking the river Teifi has long intrigued me. In this book I relate the remarkable tale of two lovers who were prepared to defy the conventions of contemporary society even after death. This volume also unearths five other historical tales ranging from the murder of Judge Johnes of Dolaucothi to the poignant events surrounding the case of Mary Prout in Pembrokeshire. The shooting of a Trawsgoed gamekeeper by Wil Cefn Coch, and its aftermath, has long been enshrined as a legend in both Cardiganshire and Ohio. The other two accounts are a complete contrast. The one reveals the strange career of Dr John Harries of Cwrtycadno, and the other the spiritual life and death of William Seward.

Bethan Phillips
March 2007

Edward Hesketh Formby's Funeral.

CHAPTER ONE

THE LOVERS' GRAVES

September 1926

Up they trudged, a motley crowd, into the lane of shadows. The men were exhausted; what had been a hard climb had now become positively dangerous. The track, scattered with sharp stones and deep ruts, was slippery, proving difficult for the two sturdy farm horses: as they slithered and strained dragging their heavy load up the steep slope, the cart jerked and creaked eerily.

The sombre procession was led by Richard Dafis, the head groom at Glandenys Mansion. He was impeccably dressed in a smart riding habit with a white cravat. A bowler hat was pulled down over a forehead glistening with beads of perspiration, for it was a clammy, murky day. The horses also felt the heat as they sweated heavily with steam rising from their flanks. Already they had pulled the red-painted *gambo* from Glandenys along the route to Llanfair Clydogau, a total distance not far off seven miles. But this last leg of the journey was no better than a narrow track with a profusion of overhanging branches brushing the cortège, their leaves caressing the highly polished Russian coffin.

However, the story leading to this bizarre funeral does not start here; its origin lies over a century earlier in another place and in very different times.

*　　　*　　　*

They arrived like conquering heroes to a rapturous welcome and the droving town of Llandovery was convulsed with expectation. Word had been out awhile that they were on their way. The clatter of hooves and barking of dogs that accompanied the cheering crowds confirmed that the drovers had indeed returned safely. The first port of call was the King's Head Inn to slake the thirst of miles upon dusty miles of those trackways that had led them from England. No one was more excited at their coming than an eager young lad of fifteen who worked at the inn. He was David Jones, the son of a local farmer. Oblivious to the exhortations of the old Vicar Prichard, the town's notable divine and poet of yesteryear, to avoid strong drink, the drovers drained their mugs of foaming ale as the young lad listened in awe to their tales of an exotic world beyond the narrow confines of Llandovery. But this was also a world full of danger where the drovers were required to keep a wary eye on their precious saddle bags, heavy with the gold and silver received in payment at Smithfield or Barnet for the Welsh Black cattle.

With his appetite for adventure whetted by these tales, David Jones yearned for the life of a drover. Although he was too young to be certificated as a drover himself, in 1780 he joined a group of drovers driving two hundred cattle to Smithfield. The journey was hard and the going difficult as they guided the herd across the narrow mountain tracks and rushing streams, seeking, if at all possible, to avoid the expense of the all-too-numerous toll gates. He very soon appreciated that droving demanded skill, enterprise and fortitude. Others who trekked alongside the drovers for protection were *merched y gerddi*. These were the young girls from west Wales who tended the gardens of the rich in London.

On reaching Smithfield Market the scene was one of sheer bedlam, with a cacophony of bellowing beasts, barking dogs, shouting and swearing dealers. This must have been the largest livestock market in the world, with an annual turnover of 250,000 cattle and 1,500,000 sheep, let alone the geese and turkeys. For a young lad from a quiet Welsh country town, the sight must have been both invigorating and intimidating. He could not have failed to notice the large amounts of money that changed hands as his canny companions from west Wales demanded nothing less than payment in gold from the dealers. Not for them the promissory notes and other bits of paper. Sovereigns could, after all, be hoarded and secreted in outhouses, chimneys, or even under beds, to ward off poverty, but they were also a source of temptation for unscrupulous robbers and highwaymen. On the return journey to Wales, David Jones was ever conscious of the tension: the drovers, their heavy saddle bags bulging, had to be constantly on their guard lest they were attacked by those wishing to steal their gold. Their corgis, so adept at controlling cattle, would sense the approaching danger, but even they would be no match for those whose vocation was theft. He never forgot this experience, and became convinced that there was a much safer way for the drovers to bring the proceeds from the sale of their animals back to Wales.

Eventually, at the age of 30, David Jones became a fully-fledged drover and soon found himself charged with the responsibility of bringing large sums of money back to Llandovery. He swiftly established a rapport with the local farmers and during the following decade his prospects were to grow steadily. They were considerably enhanced when he married Anne, the daughter of Rhys Jones, Cilrhedyn, who brought with her a substantial dowry. He was now a man of substance in his own right and could contemplate the possibility of establishing his own bank, an idea that had been germinating in his mind since his first experience of droving. Finally in 1799, he established The Black Ox Bank (Banc yr Eidion Du), which produced its own bank notes carrying the distinguishing motif of a black ox. The survival of any bank required confidence in the integrity of its founder, and David Jones was soon to acquire a trustworthy reputation. It was claimed that he 'knew more ways of making money than there are public houses in Llandovery' which was no mean feat. His banknotes could now replace the more vulnerable sovereigns previously carried by the drovers.

Fate also favoured the Black Ox Bank. In 1797, as a result of the war with France, an Order in Council suspended the redemption of the Bank of England notes. This lasted for almost twenty-five years and provided an opening for the Black Ox Bank, now trading under the name of David Jones, Llandovery. Public confidence in the bank grew apace; in 1810 an agency was established in London in co-operation with Lloyd's Bank, originally founded by the Welsh Quaker, Samuel Lloyd of Dolobran. This traded as Jones, Lloyd and Company.

A Black Ox Bank cheque.

When, in 1821, the Government rescinded the Order in Council relating to the Bank of England, many smaller banks suffered disastrous consequences. Over seventy such banks disappeared in the short space of six weeks, but not so the Black Ox Bank. The reputation for integrity built up over the years by David Jones had survived, and the confidence of clients in Jones, Lloyd and Company remained rock solid. Although the Llandovery bank had a supply of Bank of England notes, it is said that the local farmers always preferred to receive payment in Black Ox

The old Black Ox Bank, Lampeter by Robert Blayney.

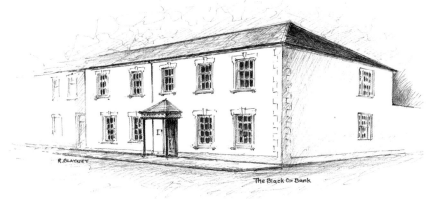

notes, such was their faith in the probity of the bank and the honesty of its founder.

With his success as a banker now assured and his wealth consolidated, David Jones soon became a local dignitary. He was appointed a Justice of the Peace and a Deputy Lieutenant. In 1825 he served as the High Sheriff for Carmarthenshire and chose as his armorial motto '*Da eich ffydd*'. By the time of his death in 1840 he had acquired a number of estates and was the owner of Blaenos, Penylan, and the more substantial property of Pantglas, and had even acquired a house in the prestigious Eaton Square in London. He also established branches of the Black Ox Bank in Llandeilo and Lampeter, and at his death his fortune was assessed at £90,000.

Despite his vast wealth, fate had dealt David Jones some cruel blows. His two sons, who were destined to expand his business, died young, so it was left to his three grandsons to shoulder the responsibility for the banks after his death. The Lampeter bank was managed by William Jones, who was to play a pivotal role in this unfolding story of unconventional love and marital infidelity. He was born in 1812, the son of John Jones, Blaenos, who had died young. Educated at Shrewsbury and then at Wadham College, Oxford, he spent some time in the London branch of Jones, Lloyd and Company acquainting himself with the business of banking. After taking up residence in Lampeter, he became friendly with the Harford family, the local squires, and lived for many years at their opulent mansion Falcondale, situated on the outskirts of the town.

Although he was still resolutely unmarried, William Jones eventually felt the need for a residence of his own. In 1855 he built Glandenys, which he described as a 'snug little mansion' a mile or so outside the town. Compared with the houses of the other local gentry, it was relatively modest, consisting of an entrance hall, a drawing room, a dining room, a morning room and a large library. It had eight principal bedrooms, the usual servants' quarters and a wine cellar. A walled kitchen-garden and numerous hothouses provided the household with an ample supply of vegetables and where more exotic fruits such as peaches and grapes were also grown. The house was completed just in time for his installation as High Sheriff of Cardiganshire in 1860. His brothers, David Jones of Pantglas and John Jones of Blaenos, also served as High Sheriffs for Carmarthenshire. Glandenys now became the venue for the lavish entertainment expected of a civic dignitary of adequate means, albeit from one who appeared to be a dyed-in-the-wool bachelor now approaching fifty years of age. The Census of 1861 provided a glimpse of the Glandenys household. William Jones himself is described as a 'banker and farmer' and his staff consisted of a cook, parlourmaid, housemaid and groom, all of whom were local and Welsh-speaking.

The grandsons of the erstwhile drover David Jones were now all actively involved in politics and, as one might expect, avid supporters of the Tory cause. David Jones of Pantglas became the Tory M.P. for Carmarthenshire. William Jones was one of the foremost supporters of Vaughan of Trawscoed, who stood as the unsuccessful Tory candidate in the seminal election of 1868 in Cardiganshire, when the Liberals made their historical breakthrough. In spite of his disappointment, he had more important concerns. His energies were now devoted almost entirely to managing the Black Ox Bank in Lampeter and expanding the legacy he had inherited from his grandfather. He also devoted himself to civic affairs and seemed content with his life as a single man of means living quietly at Glandenys.

As an astute businessman, William Jones was also intent upon expanding his assets. When Lord Carrington decided some three months before the 1868 election to sell the Llanfair estate outside Lampeter, he decided to buy it. On the estate was Llanfair Mill (Felinfawr) which had been tenanted by the same family for generations. Prior to the sale, the miller, John Morgan, had spent £200 of his own money on installing two new 'grinding stones' in order to increase the capacity of the mill. The aftermath of the 1868 election was, however, an extremely anxious time for many tenants in Cardiganshire. The Tory landlords, furious at the Liberal victory, took their revenge on those tenants who had the courage to vote for the Liberal candidate. Many were summarily ejected from their farms. John Morgan was a Liberal supporter, and on the day of the election had refused to vote for the Tory candidate, so he too feared that he would suffer for his political principles. Indeed, he asked a friend, John

Worthington of Lampeter, to visit Glandenys and plead on his behalf. In a letter written many years later, Worthington reveals the fair-minded attitude of William Jones towards his tenants.

> John Morgan asked me to approach Mr. Jones on his behalf, with a view of inducing him to allow the said John Morgan to remain at the mill, and that, if possible, at the old rent. John Morgan was a Liberal in politics, and had refused to vote at the election, and as his new landlord was a Conservative, John Morgan was afraid he would not be allowed to remain any longer at the mill. The air was full of rumours at the time at what landlords were going to do with tenants who refused to do their bidding . . . Being a well known Liberal myself, I felt somewhat reluctant to ask for an interview with Mr. Jones, but did so. He received me most kindly, and went straight to business. Mr. Jones did not refer at all to the election, or to politics or creeds; but said that John Morgan would be allowed to remain in possession of his holding like every other tenant . . . Mr. Jones generously consented to allow him to remain at the same rent, but did so most distinctly on the clear understanding that it was to be a matter of special favour, and not by any means a matter of right.

> (Evidence to Land Commission 1894)

In 1877, at the age of sixty-five, William Jones, the confirmed bachelor, shocked the neighbourhood by marrying an attractive young Englishwoman, Anne Isabel Fenton of Dalton Manor, Lancaster. She was only twenty-three years of age at the time of her wedding. The marriage, and in particular the age gap between them, inevitably intrigued the town and led to a great deal of ribald comment. But so smitten was William Jones by this exuberant and attractive young woman that he was oblivious to all such comments and criticism. In a letter to me in 1987, Miss Elizabeth Inglis Jones, the author of *Peacocks in Paradise,* whose family owned the nearby mansion of Derry Ormond, informed me that Anne Fenton's uncle rented the mansion on occasions and spent time in west Wales fishing and shooting. He was sometimes accompanied by his niece, and it was during one of those visits that she first met William Jones. A bargain was struck: she

Willliam Jones, Glandenys. In 1884 Lampeter was granted the status of a borough and William Jones served as its first mayor.

accepted his proposal of marriage on condition that she be given six fine hunters and allowed to spend some time each year away from Glandenys following the hunt. And, as a wedding present, he did indeed buy her those six valuable hunters that allowed her to indulge still further her passion for hunting. What is more, he also promised her that Glandenys would be hers after his day.

The presence of a young, vivacious wife changed the whole ambience at Glandenys. For William Jones, the staid, workaholic banker, there was a new magic in the air as he introduced this charming beauty to his friends and acquaintances. She had a most attractive personality and turned heads wherever she went. Initially, the age difference appeared to be of no consequence as he sought to indulge her every whim. Anne Jones brought colour and style to the mansion and her easy-going manner soon endeared her to those who formed the 'social set' in the county. She threw herself into all manner of community activities and was particularly fond of the local shows. Horse riding and jumping competitions were introduced and she herself proved an enthusiastic and successful competitor. Her popularity among the local gentry was quickly assured, although some must have cynically pondered the reasons why she had agreed to marry an ageing husband who had been so set in his bachelor ways. Nevertheless, with her youth and exuberance, she had become a huge social asset to her somewhat dull husband.

People soon came to marvel at her horsemanship. It was a common sight to see her riding side-saddle with great poise and dignity along the narrow lanes surrounding Glandenys. She took great pride in the fact that she was a member of the prestigious Quorn Hunt. This was the oldest fox hunt in England, established in 1753 at Quorndon Hall in Leicestershire by Hugo Meynell. Membership brought with it a social cachet which has survived to the present day, members of the Royal Family having been frequent participants, although recent legislation has now curbed the activities of such hunts. The atmosphere at the Quorn may have been more rarefied than at the rural fox hunts of the Teifi valley, but the sight of Anne Jones galloping furiously on her magnificent hunters created a frisson of excitement among the locals. Horses were her obsession, and her favourite retreats at Glandenys were the stables and the paddocks. The late Julian Cayo Evans, when owner of Glandenys, showed me the stables many years ago where the names of some of Mrs Jones's hunters could still be seen on the walls. They included the names of Black Watch, Vimmy, Spark and Juventus Eria.

Without fail, each year, Anne Jones spent many months away from Glandenys following the Quorn Hunt. Eager to indulge his young wife, her husband was willing to spend vast sums of money so that she could continue her previous activities. The horses were conveyed to Leicestershire from Llanwrda by a special train and a private carriage was set aside for her own use. She was accompanied by two members of the Glandenys staff. For the remainder of the year she appeared content to reside at the mansion, and the Census for 1881 records that William Jones, aged sixty-nine, and his wife, Anne Jones, aged twenty-seven, were in residence. The number of servants had also increased; evidence of the fact that it was no longer a bachelor's abode. While his wife spent lengthy periods away, William Jones consolidated his banking interests and, although he was by no means a landowner on the scale of the Harfords and the Inglis Joneses, he had acquired an estate of 2,744 acres with an annual rental of £1,424.

He was still eager to play a prominent role in the civic affairs of Lampeter; when, in 1884, the town was granted the status of a borough, he was elected to serve as its first mayor. This must have been the highlight of his career; with the encouragement of his young wife he was determined to ensure that his induction truly reflected this historic occasion, and would provide the town with a night to remember. The *Carmarthen Journal* of 14 November, 1884, described the occasion thus:

> Scarcely a dream was left unfulfilled. It was felt by all parties that the first meeting of the Town Council and the Election of the first Mayor should be marked by a proper commemoration of the event. It was a show of truly Victorian splendour.
>
> The day opened clear and bright for the month of November and the town presented a gay and remarkable appearance. The principal thoroughfares were spanned by arches, 8 in number, of evergreens, flags, garlands and mottoes of a complimentary character. Flags were hung at all business premises . . . There was a huge influx of people . . . There were two arches in College Street, 3 in Bridge Street, and 3 in High Street. All over the town there were flags and banners bearing the inscription 'Success to the Mayor and Mayoress – Welcome to the Corporation.' The popularity of the Mayor and his charming wife was everywhere attested to.

William Jones presented the Borough of Lampeter with a magnificent gold chain and pendant to be worn by future holders of the mayoralty. In his speech he stated that he had been a resident of the town for thirty years and trusted that a season of peace and goodwill would follow his inauguration. The new mayor and his wife then led a procession through the town, 'parading through the streets which were thronged with eager onlookers . . . a brass band played loudly and sports were held in the college field . . . An immense concourse of spectators had gathered and the Royal Artillery attended the event.'

In the evening William Jones paid for a sumptuous dinner for the Town Council and the distinguished guests at the Castle Hotel, but for the ordinary townspeople the best was yet to come. After dark, Lampeter and the surrounding countryside was ablaze with lights as the residents had been asked to place lighted candles in their windows. Then followed a display, the like of which had never before been seen in the town. Newspaper reports described the sky above as being 'lit up with exceedingly lively squibs, crackers, sky rockets, and bursting exploding stars'. It was as if the whole firmament was illuminated to honour the granting of borough status to Lampeter. Sparing no expense, the normally thrifty William Jones, urged on by his ambitious wife, had even engaged fireworks experts from the Crystal Palace to stage a grand event on the Bryn, an elevated location above the town. At 8.30pm the residents and those from the surrounding countryside who had thronged the town, were treated to a pyrotechnic display of fantastic designs normally arranged only for royal occasions. The spectators gasped when, one after another, variegated colours flamed across the sky then fell to earth in shimmering showers of sparks. A vertical wheel produced a perfect circle of fire with a coloured centre, and a huge silver fountain poured forth glittering streams of differing colours. At one point a brilliant sun lit up the town and simulated garden designs of lilac and laburnum blossoms appeared. Jewel-headed cobras threaded the sky and a rocket discharged a display of writhing snakes. As the spectators stood transfixed, there seemed no end to the wonders, when suddenly, a jack-in-the-box appeared in the sky exploding with fantastical effect. After hours of spectacular entertainment, the finale took place in Harford Square at midnight, where a massive balloon ascended, lighting up every nook and cranny of the town. This night was to be talked about for years to come and, for William Jones and his wife, it was a triumphant introduction to their year in office.

An aerial view of Glandenys Mansion.

Although Glandenys was a modest estate in comparison with others in the county, both William Jones and his wife were keen to promote new agricultural techniques and to assist their tenant farmers. In 1877, William had become the first president of the Lampeter Agricultural Society. By 1887, the Lampeter Agricultural Show had become an annual event. This gave Mrs Jones further opportunies to display her equestrian skills. A show-jumping competition was introduced, and every year she treated crowds thronging the event to a thrilling exhibition of the art. It was reported that 'She delighted the packed audience who loudly clapped and cheered as she cleared the high gates and ten foot water jumps on her magnificent hunter. With her glamour and elegance she stole the highlight of the show'. Anne Jones revelled in the adulation heaped upon her, and the tradition of showjumping was to remain a feature of the Lampeter Show up until the present day.

His marriage had provided William Jones with a much admired consort, but something was missing: it had not produced a son and heir to inherit the famous Black Ox Bank. The prospect of this was now fast receding, causing William Jones a great deal of concern. His elder brother David had long since died and his younger brother John was ailing. He had assiduously devoted his early years to promoting the Black Ox Bank and, ever conscious of his grandfather's achievements, he had been desperate to ensure that it continued within the family. But, too late in life, he realised that money could not buy everything, least of all a child. Anne Jones, however, did not appear to share his sense of urgency. Her life was full, as she immersed herself in country activities and social events. The Census of 1891 suggests that she had even acquired a knowledge of Welsh so that she could converse with the tenants and labourers, the vast majority of whom are recorded as monoglot Welsh speakers. According to the record of those residing at Glandenys we have the following:

Name		Language
William Jones	aged 79	English and Welsh
Anne Jones	aged 37	English and Welsh

The members of staff consisted of John Edwards, butler, Freddie Mills, gardener, and John Jones, coachman, all from Lampeter. The cook came from Scotland and one of the housemaids came from Westmoreland, but the other maids were local.

Throughout her marriage Anne Jones never missed her annual visit to the Quorn Hunt, but in January 1892, this particular visit was to have unforeseen consequences. During her lengthy stay away from Glandenys, she met a much younger man, Edward Hesketh Formby, a young lawyer from a distinguished family of Liverpool solicitors, who was also a keen follower of the hunt and an Oxford graduate. An accomplished sportsman, he shared many of Anne Jones's own interests in country pursuits. Although at the age of only twenty-three, he was fourteen years younger, they became instantly attracted to one another. Up until that point, Anne appears to have been a loyal and dutiful wife to William Jones, but things were set to change dramatically.

In March 1892, Anne invited Edward Formby to visit west Wales. For the sake of propriety he stayed at Derry Ormond, the mansion of the Inglis-Jones family. In her letter to me, Miss Elisabeth Inglis Jones recalled some of his subsequent visits and his developing relationship with Anne Jones.

> . . . This has taken me back to the days of my youth – when Mrs Jones and Mr Formby were often driving along in a very smart dog cart on their way to go fishing at Llanfair. I remember Mr Formby with ginger side whiskers and dressed in very loud checks. He paid Mrs Jones long visits . . . At first she had a lady companion as a chaperone . . . and all was as it should be!! However, in due course the chaperone was dispensed with and Mr. Formby settled down there for good.

From the beginning William Jones must have felt somewhat uneasy, but he agreed that Formby could visit his wife at Glandenys, providing that they were accompanied by a lady companion to act as a chaperone. At first Formby continued to stay at Derry Ormond, but the relationship soon blossomed into a fully-fledged love affair. The couple were already exchanging intimate letters, with the Glandenys coachman acting as the courier. For this service he was paid one penny for each letter. Soon the affair between Mrs Jones and her young paramour became the talk of the locality, if not the county.

Anne Jones cared not a fig about the burgeoning scandal. She had always revealed herself as a strong, independent character intent upon ploughing her own furrow. Having dispensed with her lady companion, she invited Formby to move to Glandenys and he eagerly grasped the opportunity. William Jones, the much respected banker, now found himself in a *ménage à trois*. So besotted was his wife with Formby, that she was deaf to any of his entreaties to end the affair. And so besotted was Jones with his charismatic young wife, and so reliant upon her companionship and social accomplishments, that the prospect of living without her was not one which William Jones at his time in life could contemplate. Having indulged most of her whims throughout his marriage, he preferred to see Formby living at Glandenys rather than lose his wife completely. After all, there was always the prospect that Formby, who was still a young man, would eventually grow weary of the company of an older woman and return to the family's law practice in Liverpool.

Unfortunately, life seldom follows a rational path and for the next few years Anne Jones managed to enjoy what was, for her, the best of both worlds. In many respects it was a farcical situation. She continued to support her ageing and by now ailing husband in his civic duties, although everyone knew where her true affections lay. We can but conjecture the feelings of William Jones himself, confronted daily by the presence of Formby at Glandenys. Did he regret his rashness in marrying, at the age of sixty-five, a wife so much younger than himself? Jane Austen may well have written that 'it is a truth universally acknowledged that a single man in possession of a good fortune must be in want of a wife,' but she was less forthcoming about the wisdom of such a want. William Jones may well have started to have misgivings.

There is little doubt that when, at the age of twenty-three, Anne Jones had agreed to marry the stolid, elderly, Welsh banker, she had been enchanted by the prospect of a comfortable country life and a licence to indulge her passion for horses. Hers was, however, an instinctively free spirit and her meeting with Formby released that spirit irresistibly. She would no longer be a caged bird bound by the norms of respectability: she would follow the impulses of her new-found love and passion. After all, she was still a youngish forty-year-old trapped in marriage to an increasingly frail husband approaching the age of eighty-two.

Flouting public opinion, Anne Jones and Formby spent hours in each other's company, shooting on the estate, fishing on the banks of the Teifi, and riding with total abandon along the narrow country lanes. They continued to attend the Quorn Hunt together and were increasingly being regarded as a couple. Naturally, all this was to prove profoundly embarrassing for William Jones. He felt ridiculed and

Llanfair Clydogau Show Poster, 1919.

abused and the situation was to have an adverse affect on his health. The future of the Black Ox Bank, an institution that he had devoted his life to enhance, also troubled him. He had not managed to produce a direct heir and both his brothers were by now dead. The charming bride, to whom he had promised so much, was now in the arms of a young lover. Fearful that his wealth would be squandered, he secretly made a new will leaving the bulk of his estate to his nephew Gerwyn Jones of Pantglas, the son of his eldest brother, David. After her husband's day, the future of Anne Jones and Formby, as occupants of Glandenys, would depend upon the goodwill of his nephew.

At the age of eighty-four, William Jones's health was far from robust. All the certainties of his life were in danger of vanishing. In November, 1896, while his wife and Formby were indulging themselves in the excitement of the Quorn Hunt, William was advised to visit Bournemouth for the sake of his health. Accompanied by his butler, his coachman and a maid, he undertook what must have been for him a long and arduous journey. It was with a sense of impending doom that he left the mansion which had been his home for nigh on half a century.

He stayed at the Haven Hotel on the seafront at Bournemouth, hoping that a release from the tensions at Glandenys, the bracing sea air, and the walks along the beaches, would do him good. As the New Year approached, there was a distinct chill in the air making it impossible for him to venture out; unfortunately, 1897 brought with it a harsh spell of winter cold. January can be a cruel month, particularly so for a sick old man like William Jones. Although he was constantly attended by his devoted servants and under the care of doctors, it was evident that his life was slowly ebbing away. He longed to return to west Wales, but he was now becoming too weak to contemplate the long journey. The struggle at Glandenys between youth and old age had been too much for him. As he lay in a hotel in Bournemouth, one wonders whether his mind was filled with hatred for his wife, or was he able to forgive her and call to mind those halcyon days when as a young bride she brought colour and zest to the rather grey life of an ageing bachelor? We shall never know. His great ambition had been to perpetuate his grandfather's legacy, but he had been denied even this. Apparently, his constant prayer had been 'Pray God give me health till my work is done.'

On 7 January, at the age of 85, he finally passed away at the Haven
Hotel, Bournemouth. He was a wealthy man, but he had died a
disillusioned soul. His dream of passing on the Black Ox Bank to a son
was unfulfilled, and his wish for a comfortable and untroubled old age
at Glandenys had been shattered. He had not even been granted his
undoubted wish of dying in his own bed in his own home, but had
drawn his last breath in an anonymous hotel room in an English seaside
resort in mid-winter, without the comfort of his own wife at his bedside.

His death was widely reported in the press. The *Western Mail* of 8
January, 1897 referred to him as

> one of the best known Gentlemen . . . who was a senior partner in the
> firm of David Jones & Co. Bankers at Llandovery, Llandeilo and
> Lampeter . . . a staunch Conservative and a brother of Mr John Jones
> Blaenos who represented the County of Carmarthen as a Conservative
> for many years . . . Mr. Gerwyn Jones of Pantglas will inherit the
> greater part of his vast property.

His civic achievements are listed and there is but one brief reference to
his wife.

> Mr. Jones late in life married Anne Fenton of Dalton Manor in
> Lancashire and leaves no issue.

His lonely return to Lampeter was by an overnight train arriving at
7.30am. At the station his coffin was met by friends and relatives and,
as a mark of respect, the blinds of the houses and businesses in the town
were drawn as it was carried to Glandenys. The exterior of the Black
Ox Bank in High Street was completely decked with black mourning
ribbon. He was buried on 12 January, 1897 and on the day of his
funeral, a short service was conducted at the mansion by the Reverend
J.N. Evans. The cortège then proceeded to Llanfair Clydogau church
where the Dean of Gloucester, who was married to his niece, conducted
the service in the church. At the graveside the Reverend Daniel Jones of
Lampeter conducted the concluding service in Welsh. A huge throng of
mourners surrounded the church testifying to the fact that the deceased
had been a greatly respected figure in the town and beyond.

The lonely grave of William Jones, long stripped of its original splendour.

pic. Tim Jones

With the death of the three brothers, the fortunes of the Black Ox Bank were now in the hands of William Jones's nephew, Gerwyn Jones, but he had neither the acumen nor the dedication of the founder's grandsons. But what of the future for Anne Jones and Formby? The ownership of Glandenys and its effects had now passed to Gerwyn Jones who must have been uneasy about the treatment afforded to his uncle in his declining years. William Jones had died a comparatively rich man leaving the sum of £33,974 - 6s - 6d in cash and a substantial estate. Gerwyn Jones himself was already a wealthy landowner having inherited the vast Pantglas estate, and now he was President of the three Black Ox Banks. Within the family of William Jones, Anne Jones and her lover were now pariahs. When Viola Davies-Evans of Highmead, Gerwyn Jones's niece, married in September, 1897, the names of the great and the good within the counties of Carmarthenshire and Cardiganshire were on the guest list. A notable exception is the name of Anne Jones of Glandenys, although the bride's mother had been William Jones's niece.

Even taking into account her errant behaviour during the final years of the marriage, she must have been sorely disappointed by the terms of the will, but with the help of her lawyer lover she was determined to fight hard for the right to remain at the mansion. Gerwyn Jones himself had no need of Glandenys, for his mansion at Pantglas was much more substantial. According to all accounts, he took very little personal interest in his estates, preferring to leave his business affairs in the hands of his nephew, Colonel Herbert Davies-Evans of Highmead. Although he acted as High Sheriff and Deputy Lieutenant for Carmarthenshire, he was very much a playboy, preferring to spend his time in London and abroad, only returning to Wales for the shooting season. David Jones the Drover would have turned in his grave at the prospect of his descendants squandering the wealth he had so assiduously built up and neglecting the banks he had founded. The 1901 Census shows that the sole occupant of Glandenys at the time was John Edwards, the butler, who probably acted as a caretaker. We have no record of Anne Jones and Formby living there. The census shows that the surrounding mansions of Derry Ormond, Falcondale and Llanllŷr were thriving households whereas Glandenys appears to have been an empty ghost of a place. The mystery remains regarding Anne Jones and Formby's situation after Gerwyn Jones inherited Glandenys. Within two years, however, tragedy was to strike. On 20 September, 1903, the high-living Gerwyn Jones died suddenly at the Grosvenor Hotel, London.

According to the *Carmarthen Journal* he was only ill for a few days and the cause of death was pneumonia. It was noted that 'he preferred the more active life of London when not travelling the world as was his wont.' He was given a grand funeral and the mourners were drawn from the notable families of west Wales, but the name of Mrs Anne Jones is again absent. His will reveals the extent of Gerwyn Jones's wealth. He left effects valued at £128,769-17s-1d, together with the mansions of Pantglas, Blaenos and Glandenys. Unmarried and with no issue, he left his estate to his sister Mary Eleanor, the wife of Col. Herbert Davies-Evans of Highmead. The management of the Black Ox Banks now became the responsibility of this family. The banks were managed by Col. Davies – Evans's sons, Delme and Herbert, who had no real experience of banking. In 1909, the inevitable occurred when the bank was taken over by Lloyds Bank Ltd. It was not what David Jones the founder would have wished, or indeed, what William Jones would have wanted, but time and events eclipse everything. One of the great historical banks of Wales had lost its independence, but as a gesture to its past glory, the figure of the Black Ox continued to feature on the cheques of the Llandovery branch for many years to come.

But what of the fortunes of Mrs Anne Jones? No shrinking violet, she had continued to assert her right to live at Glandenys. An accommodation of a kind was reached with the new heirs of the estate, and she resumed her occupancy of the mansion accompanied by her lover, Formby. It appears that she was granted a life tenancy which would have terminated at her death or been nullified in the event of her remarrying. Her social standing had not been diminished after her husband's death. Elisabeth Inglis Jones in her letter testified to this:

> Her aura of glamour never failed to win over the locals, and she became a popular Lady of the Manor, throwing herself into local events with gusto.

Glandenys after the fire.

BURIALS in the Parish of *Llanfair Clydoge* in the County of *Cardigan* in the Year 18*96*				
Margaret Davies No. 733.	Penbryn	Oct: 1st 1896	1 month	J. N. Evans B.a Vicar
John Rees No. 734.	Blaenau Cellan	Nov 12th 1896	87 years	J. N. Evans B.a Vicar
William Jones No. 735.	Glandenys Silian	Jan: 12th 1897	85 years	J.N. Evans B.a. Vicar. Daniel Jones m.a. Vicar of Lampeter. H.D.M. Spence D.D. Dean of Gloucester
Thomas Williams No. 736.	Llandovery Clungunford (J.N.E)	Jan: 22nd 1897	20 years	J. N. Evans Vicar

William Jones's Death Certificate.

Although poor William Jones might have devoutly wished that his young rival would return to his Liverpool roots, Formby had quickly settled into the life of a country squire, and saw no reason to turn his back on it. It was far preferable to the claustrophobic atmosphere of a lawyer's office. Chance had brought him to west Wales and it had provided him with an ideal life's companion. Together they could follow an idyllic way of life, sharing the same interests. Elisabeth Inglis Jones recalled that their great delight was fishing for trout, sewin and salmon which, at that time, would have been plentiful in the river. They would spend endless hours on the river bank enjoying the ever-changing kaleidoscope of nature where nothing stood still.

Formby, in particular, regarded himself as an exemplary fisherman and had equipped himself with the most expensive fishing tackle. According to those who could recall him fishing the Teifi, he was, nevertheless, frequently outwitted by the local poachers. Much to his annoyance, they, with their microscopic knowledge of the river, knew where the most favourable stretches were. With this knowledge, they could venture forth at night and return home with a particularly fine salmon. They were clever enough to evade the bailiffs, and, on occasions, they would nail the tail of a salmon to the door of the head bailiff as a gesture of defiance. Not for them the expensive rods used by Formby, for they were experts at gaffing or tickling a fish, and their catches ensured that their families were well fed when times were lean.

During his Oxford days, Formby was an accomplished athlete and throughout his life sought to maintain a high level of fitness. He was also an excellent shot and possessed the most expensive guns which were much envied by his shooting companions. To satisfy his interest in this sport he bred two hundred pheasants annually at Tanygraig, the home farm of the estate; with an unerring eye, it was claimed that he hardly ever missed a bird in flight. Anne Jones retained her obsession with horses and even the advancing years did nothing to diminish this. She was still a fearless rider who turned out in all weather. The locals came to recognise the sound of the thundering hoof beats of her hunters sending the mud flying as she rode like Jehu along the narrow lanes, her hair flying in the wind. Her hunters were the children she never had.

But on February 29, 1908, calamity struck: Glandenys mansion was severely damaged by a fire which started in a chimney. The fire was discovered in the library during the afternoon by one of the servants and the contents of the room were soon ablaze. The flames could be seen for miles around, and crowds of people rushed from Lampeter to witness the disastrous occurrence. It was the most spectacular sight since the display of pyrotechnics which followed the inauguration of William Jones as the first mayor of the borough. Lampeter's fire brigade would now be put to the test. The brigade consisted of volunteers drawn from the townspeople and the College students. In 1904, they had resigned en bloc because of the reluctance of the Council to pay for adequate equipment. There had been some improvements, but their training still consisted of practices held once every quarter. Nevertheless, they reached Glandenys in good time, and as the *Western Mail* recorded, they worked valiantly in an attempt to save the mansion and its contents.

> Captain Richard John was able to start the fire engine and reached the scene shortly after five o'clock. A brook nearby supplied ample water, and Captain John directed the hose to the burning building. The fire was increasing in intensity every moment, and the huge tongues of flame directed their work of destruction towards the other portions of the residence. The excited inmates, assisted by scores of willing helpers, worked like Trojans to save the beautiful and expensive furniture. The library is situated in the middle of the mansion, and the fire aided by a strong wind, worked in both directions. The brigade was thus greatly handicapped but they kept pouring on volumes of water . . . The mansion is in the occupation of Mrs Jones, widow of the late Mr William Jones, first mayor of Lampeter and one of the founders of the Old Bank.

The report adds that Mrs Jones was away at the time visiting friends in Nantwich, Cheshire, but that the place was 'in charge of Mr Formby.' On her return to Glandenys, Anne Jones must have been devastated as she surveyed the wreckage of the mansion which was, according to the *Western Mail* reporter, a 'mass of ruins with valuable suites of furniture destroyed.' The only source of comfort was that, mercifully, nobody had been hurt and the treasured hunters had been taken to a place of safety. The mansion had been rendered uninhabitable and would require extensive rebuilding. Anne Jones and Formby would now need a temporary home, so they decided to move to Tanygraig, the home farm, in order to keep an eye on the restoration work at the mansion. Adaptations were swiftly put in train to meet their needs. A new porch was built, the ceilings raised in a bedroom, the living room was extended and wooden shutters were installed. Nemesis seemed to have struck, but the lovers were determined that their congenial lifestyle should be restored as soon as possible.

Eventually Glandenys was rebuilt, but Thomas Lloyd, a foremost authority on Welsh houses, is of the view that the restored mansion was only a pale shadow of the original building which was a kind of 'junior Pantglas.'

Formby had found rural contentment in this corner of Wales, but he had also found something else. He and Anne became obsessed with one particular spot known as Bryncysegrfan – 'the hill of the sacred place'. This was located on a wooded mountain slope overlooking the Teifi valley, and in times past, it must, as the name suggested, have had a special significance. Tradition held that at one time it was an ancient burial ground, and that the bodies still lying there were protected by benign spirits sheltering in the trees. Formby was so fascinated by the aura of mystery and myth surrounding the spot, that he bought an old cottage called Tanybryn which stood nearby. It was originally a *tŷ unnos* or a rudely-made cottage built in one night. He was also anxious to acquire the plot of land attached to the cottage, and in 1923, he prevailed upon a neighbour, Mrs Hannah Thomas, Gwarffordd, to sell it to him. Although Formby and Anne Jones were delighted with their purchase, their friends and neighbours thought them mad to have bought land in such a barren, windswept spot. Little did they know what really lay behind this decision.

From the top of the hill they could take in the whole sweep of the Teifi valley with its morning curtain of mists and its glistening pools. It was here that Formby and Anne Jones entered into a special covenant. Both were captivated by the spot, and here they felt in harmony with the spirits of those who had been buried in this sacred earth; they felt its healing quality and were overwhelmed by its magical and mysterious atmosphere. Formby also sought the ancient paths and absorbed the local legends and superstitions. Not far away was Sarn Helen, the Roman road where the legions had tramped on their way from Carmarthen to the fort at Llanio. They had often galloped furiously along its straight stretches past Carreg y Bwci, a name that suggests a link with a long lost world of pagan rituals. Formby had become convinced that on Bryncysegrfan he and his lover could be at one with this mythical past. Elisabeth Inglis Jones mentioned that he was a deeply cultured person, obsessed with antiquity. He had already indicated that he was prepared to defy convention, but now he was to go much further. Unknown to his neighbours, he had already determined that when his time came he would wish to be buried here. Although it was unconsecrated ground, he felt that here he had found an eternal resting place from which emanated a peace which was beyond the power of words.

By 1926, Formby had lived in the area for over thirty years and he and Anne Jones were by now part of the landscape. Their relationship had long been accepted and they had achieved a large measure of respectability. Within the community they were acknowledged as the lord and the lady of the manor. But life is fragile and a veil of sorrow was soon to descend upon their blissful world. Towards the end of August 1926, the normally fit and healthy Formby began to feel unwell. After a brief illness he died on 2 September at the age of 60. In his will he bequeathed all his worldly goods, amounting to £2862-5s-8d, to Anne Jones; in it he referred to her as 'my bright little friend and the love of my life.'

As was to be expected, Anne Jones, crushed by grief, was inconsolable. Gone forever were the days of lust and what had been so sweet was now turned to dust. Theirs had been an intensely emotional affair which had survived periods of universal censure, but had remained rooted in a deep and everlasting love. Now its glow had been forever diminished to be replaced by the sharp pangs of sorrow and Anne was faced with the ordeal of arranging Formby's funeral. Accounts of his death appeared in the papers, describing him as a keen athlete, a sportsman of distinction, a fishing and shooting enthusiast and

Burial in the Parish of ...Llangian... Clynnog... .... in the County of ...Caernarvon... ...., in the year 19.2.6...

No.	Name.	Abode.	When Buried.	Age.	By whom the Ceremony was performed.
241	Maria Richard	Beulah Llanfair Clydogau	May 29th 1926	76 years	J. N. Evans Vicar
242	Edward Hesketh Formby	[at] Glandwy Silian Buried at Tanygroes Plot Llanfair Parish	Sep 6th 1926	60 years	J. N. Evans Vicar J. H. Davies Vicar of Silian
243	David James	Abermalais Cwll an	Oct 20th 1926	92 years	J. N. Evans Vicar

Edward Hesketh Formby's Death Certificate.

an Oxford Blue in rowing and athletics. But much more publicity was to follow when it was realised that Anne Jones was to arrange a funeral strictly in accordance with his expressed wishes. She would follow his instructions to the letter and arrange for him to be buried on the remote parcel of mountain land on Bryncysegrfan, which had meant so much to both of them.

Formby had given detailed instructions and decreed that his body should be placed in a polished oak coffin of Russian design and that his fishing tackle and his precious Purdy guns be buried with him. The coffin was to be carried on a red-painted farm cart, red being the Glandenys estate colour. There would be no flowers, but he wished the cart to be covered with soft moss and heather and drawn by his two favourite farm horses, Derby and Dame Gelda. As the news of the arrangements for his interment spread, the press took an increasing interest and headlines such as these appeared in the newspapers: *Mountain Top Burial, Old Blue's Lone Grave, A Sportsman's Funeral.* Inevitably, the funeral became the talk of the locality. Many facetiously maintained that he had chosen this elevated spot in order to keep an eye on those who were wont to poach his salmon in the Teifi. They could not comprehend his wish to be buried on this remote patch of land, for it was certainly not what they would have wished for their nearest and dearest. To the local people it was a place steeped in superstition, where the sighing of the wind in the trees was akin to the voices of long dead ancestors.

On the day of the funeral, crowds had gathered along the route to be taken, all agog with excitement. After a short service at Glandenys, the farm cart or *gambo* pulled by the two horses set out; alongside trudged six bearers drawn from the ranks of the servants and tenants of the estate. The seven-mile journey was a gruelling one following a tortuous route over Llangybi mountain before descending into the village of Llanfair Clydogau. On the narrow bridge at Llanfair crowds had assembled and the cortège halted for a brief moment so that they could pay their respects. At the nearby Llanfair church where, ironically, William Jones had been laid to rest those many years ago, Anne Jones and her sister stepped from their carriage and entered for a brief service. They were met at the door by the Inglis Jones family of Derry Ormond and many other representatives of the county families including Colonel

Powell of Nanteos and Colonel Dudley Drummond, agent of the Glandenys estate. From the door they would have glimpsed the white marble gravestone of William Jones surrounded by iron railings standing as a stark reminder of the drama and intrigue which had served as a backdrop to this story.

It was not customary for women to attend the final interment, which in this case was just as well, for the final leg was to be a never-forgotten experience, in particular for the bearers. So began the arduous ascent up an impossibly difficult and narrow cart-track to the spot where a grave had been prepared. Dangerous potholes and sharp stones littered the lane causing the horses to slither and slide. The cart lurched and swayed as it rumbled on. So dense was the foliage overhanging it, that the servants had to cut the branches of hazel, birch and willow which slapped the ornate coffin. The horses, now clearly exhausted, plodded on reluctantly at a snail's pace as they grew ever nearer to the spot chosen by Formby as his final resting-place. The bearers who had accompanied the coffin from Glandenys were so close to a state of

David Pugh preparing for Edward Hesketh Formby's Funeral.

collapse that the head groom feared for their safety. With the crowds of curious onlookers behind the hedges fighting for the most suitable vantage points, it was in danger of becoming more of a carnival than a dignified burial. When the cortège reached Tanybryn, Formby's humble retreat, the bearers had to remove the coffin from the cart and carry it shoulder high over layers of loose stone walls, through clinging brambles and thick undergrowth to reach the grave. Several times the men lost their footing on what had become practically a vertical incline.

One newspaper reporter described the funeral thus:

> on a steep side of Mynydd Cysegrfan, a mountain in a wild romantic spot . . . the last part of the route was very steep and his body had to be carried by the tenants and servants of the estate.

The *Western Mail* reported that

> The last part of the route was so steep that his body had to be taken off the cart and carried by the tenants and servants to be laid in a simple unbricked grave with no epitaph.

Finally, Edward Hesketh Formby had been laid in the unpretentious grave of his choice with his feet facing the river Teifi. On his coffin, in deference to his wishes, they laid his precious Purdy guns wrapped in sackcloth and also his favourite fishing rods. As they lowered the coffin into the ground, many of those who had carried it were physically exhausted and must have heaved a sigh of relief. As the gravediggers toiled, shovelling earth and stones on the coffin, some among the onlookers were already contemplating the possibility of retrieving the valuable guns and rods. A week or so later, two young local lads who had watched the proceedings made their way one dark night through the thick undergrowth surrounding the grave armed with shovels. Their objective was to retrieve the guns and the rods. As they were about to start digging, the silence was broken by a loud unearthly screeching noise and a large white owl flew out of a nearby tree with its wings flapping. The boys were so frightened by this apparition that they threw down their shovels and scampered away from the grave as fast as their legs could carry them. The branches tore at their clothes and the brambles scratched their legs, but they did not stop until they reached the main road. Bloodied and terrified they made their way home. The following night they summoned up enough courage to collect their shovels, but they never visited the grave again.

Edward Hesketh Formby and Mrs Anne Jones, Glandenys.

As would have been expected of one of her social standing, Anne Jones bore herself with a stoical dignity during the funeral, but ahead lay a period of painful mourning. As long as Formby was by her side, she had felt secure. Their lives had been driven by the strength of their affection for each other and they had vowed that neither time nor distance, nor even the power of death would ever separate them. Nevertheless, she was now confronted with the reality of her loss and, during the early days following his death, she was overwhelmed by grief. Many an afternoon was spent weeping at his graveside, recollecting all the things they had done together and yearning for those distant Arcadian days of contentment. Throughout the autumn, as the trees shed their leaves over the grave, there was no escape from the sadness of her situation and from the void that had been left in her life. She could not even bring herself to take an interest in her magnificent hunters, for so long her pride and joy.

The response to suffering is ultimately a measure of inner fortitude, and Anne Jones had in the past shown that she possessed this in plenty. She gradually determined to reclaim her zest for living; although, at the age of 75, she could no longer be the accomplished rider galloping with her hair flowing in the wind, captivating her many admirers. But according to Elisabeth Inglis Jones, she now resorted to wearing a golden wig, and with highly rouged cheeks, she tried to recapture some of her youthful allure. From a distance she still appeared 'as a slight young girl.' She sought to resume some of her former responsibilities as the mistress of Glandenys by participating in the local shows, particularly the one held at Llanfair where she was Life President; she was even made a President of the Lampeter Football Club. Her age did not deter her from continuing to follow the local hunts and, as the season for the Quorn Hunt beckoned, she once again prepared for the trek to Leicestershire. Although the absence of Formby made it a bitter-sweet experience, her spirits would be buoyed by the company of so many old friends during the Christmas season. Before leaving Glandenys, her last thoughts were of Formby, when she arranged for Hannah Thomas, Gwarffordd, to look after the grave in her absence. Here she had found both tranquillity and sadness, but her lover's death would always remain an open wound that would never heal.

For the next three years, Anne Jones made the best of her situation, immersing herself in local activities and supporting charitable causes. Her precious hunters were still her pride and joy. When they became too old to serve their purpose, she reluctantly had to ask the groom to put them down, for she could not bear to see them suffering. They were buried with dignity and did not end up as meat for the hounds. The loss of Formby had been a cruel blow and it was starting to impact upon her general health. Nevertheless, in spite of this and despite her advanced age, she was determined to carry on; to that end she decided to attend the Christmas meeting of the Quorn Hunt in 1928. This was to prove her final visit, for on her return she was taken ill and the diagnosis was heart failure. She was visited regularly by Dr Evan Evans of Lampeter, but it was to no avail. Deprived of the companionship of Formby and now too weak to follow her favourite pastimes, she lost the will to live. After an illness of almost three months, she passed away peacefully at Glandenys on 21 March, 1929, aged seventy-eight. Elisabeth Inglis Jones recalled that she died in her sleep as the dawn was breaking over the Teifi valley on the first day of spring, just as the primroses were lighting up the hedgerows surrounding the mansion. She summed up Anne Jones's relationship with Formby thus:

> Their love did not seem to alter with time . . . first Formby died and Mrs Jones soon followed him. Theirs had been an abiding passion which never seemed to wane.

The question of her funeral arrangements now presented themselves. In spite of her long-standing liaison with her lover, she was still the widow of William Jones of the Black Ox Bank who lay in the cemetery at Llanfair Clydogau. Her published will subsequently revealed that she was a wealthy person in her own right and this may account for the degree of independence she exhibited throughout her life. She left effects to the value of £92,130-15s-1d and probate was granted to Sir Francis Dudley Williams-Drummond. Her death was recorded in the *Western Mail* where she was described as

> a lady of prepossessing appearance and a very prominent figure in society circles in west Wales. She was a most capable horse rider and kept and trained several hunters which she skilfully rode at the Quorn Hunt in Leicestershire, which many of the Royal Family frequent.

But the intriguing question of her burial was the main interest for the press. The *Western Mail* continued:

> she held unusual views with regard to funeral ceremonies and left instructions as to the manner in which her own obsequies were to be carried out – one of which was that no mourning was to be worn.

It soon became clear that her instructions went further than this, for she had resolved that she would not lie alongside her husband at Llanfair

Clydogau but that she wished to be buried on Bryncysegrfan with Formby. In life she had thrown convention to the wind; in death she was determined to follow suit. The arrangements for her funeral were to mirror those of Formby. The newspapers reported her funeral in detail and the *Cambrian News* chronicled the events thus:

> Buried on a Hillside
> Lampeter Lady
> Favourite Hunters at Funeral
> Carried on a gambo painted red, the estate colours, and accompanied by her hunters, the remains of Mrs Ann Isabel Jones, Glandenys were conveyed to their last resting place at Bryncysegrfan on the hillside between Llanfair and Llanddewi-brefi . . . She was the widow of William Jones (of David Jones & Co., Banc yr Eidion Du, Lampeter) and was a native of Lancashire

No mention is made of her relationship with Formby.

On the day of the funeral a torrent of mourners swept along the fields and the lanes. They included the tenants, farm labourers and also the inquisitive bystanders who were curious to witness yet again an unconventional burial. It was so unlike the traditional Welsh *angladd* with its long drawn-out ritual of lengthy prayers, sermons and sorrowful hymns sung by black-suited mourners. As desired by the deceased, the arrangements were to follow strictly those for the burial of Edward Hesketh Formby less than three years previously. The casket was again to be of a Russian design with brass fittings and the *gambo* was again painted red and covered with moss and wild flowers. Mrs Jones had expressed a wish to be buried in her hunting attire, and that the *gambo* be drawn by two of her horses, Aeroplane and Dame Gelda. It was also her wish that it be followed by two of her favourite hunters, Vimmy and Black Watch. No mourning clothes were to be worn; in deference to her wishes the stud groom was clad in hunting attire and the head keeper in his working clothes. The route to be followed was similar to the one followed by Formby's funeral. It went through the village of Llangybi and then followed a circuitous route with a steep incline to Llanfair Clydogau church, It was met at the door of the church by Mr and Mrs Inglis Jones of Derry Ormond, their daughter Elisabeth and other

Burial in the Parish of ...Llanfair Clydogan... in the County of ...Cardigan... in the year 1929.

No.	Name.	Abode.	When Buried.	Age.	By whom the Ceremony was performed.
268	Annie Isabel Jones *	Glaudeng's, Silian	March 25th 1929	78 years	J. N. Evans Vicar
269	Martha Jane	Bryn-glas Llanfair	April 6th 1929	60 years	J. N. Evans Vicar
270	Mary Griffiths	16 College Street Lampeter	April 16th 1929	80 years	D. W. Thomas Vicar of Lampeter

* Buried in enclosed plot, near Pêas, Llanfair Clydogan Parish.

Death certificate of Mrs Anne Jones.

Richard Dafis, the head groom, on the day of Mrs Jones's funeral, ready to lead the grim procession.

friends. At Llanfair Clydogau, the tenants of the Glandenys estate lined the bridge over the Teifi and the children from the local school stood at the church gate as a mark of respect.

The cortège came to a stop and the casket was taken into the church for a brief service conducted by the Vicar. Outside, stood the *gambo* with the two sturdy farm horses held by Richard Dafis, the head groom. They were already sweating profusely after pulling it along the exhausting route from Glandenys. Behind them, the two handsome hunters champed impatiently at their bits as they were held by the second groom. Inside the church were assembled many representatives of the county families, including Captain Powell of Nanteos, testifying to the fact that the deceased's unconventional lifestyle had been accepted by the gentry. The principal mourner was her sister Mrs Miller, but also present was Mrs Davies-Evans of Highmead. This showed that the relationship between her and the family of her late husband William

Jones had improved over the years Even so, the irony of the situation cannot have escaped them all as Mrs Jones's funeral had to pass her late husband's grave on its way to Bryncysegrfan. None of the women attended the final committal, so they were spared the Everest-style ascent to the graveside. The *Cambrian News* reporter recorded that

> The sight of the horses drawing the gambo up the steep incline was one never to be forgotten. At the graveside situated in a rugged spot overlooking the river Teifi and enclosed by walls of loose stone, the committal rites were performed.

It was a simple but moving ceremony. The Vicar, the Rev. J.N. Evans, recited in sonorous tones, 'The earth is the Lord's and the fullness thereof, the earth and everything that dwells therein.' Anne Jones had wanted nothing more.

Before the coffin lid was finally closed, there was one more intriguing gesture. Mr Hands, her solicitor from Loughborough, placed a sealed envelope in the coffin in accordance with Mrs Jones's final wishes. Apparently, she had requested in the last days of her life that this be done, but absolutely no one was to know its contents. The coffin was then screwed down and lowered gently into the moss-lined grave. As the two gravediggers proceeded to shovel earth and stones which clattered onto the polished, expensive Russian casket, an unnatural silence and stillness descended over the whole scene; even the birds stopped singing. Her day was finally done. The lovers were now united for eternity. Tolstoy once said that 'to live your life is not as simple as to cross a field.' So it was in the complicated lives of William Jones, his wife Anne and her paramour Edward Hesketh Formby. Sadly, after her death, her favourite hunters were shot in accordance with her instructions. She could not be parted from them even in death. This was not an untoward happening: Charles Dickens had also ordered that his favourite pony be put down after his day.

It is a sad thing to witness the sale of a deceased person's personal effects and to see them exposed to the curious gaze of those seeking a bargain. So it must have been when the personal possessions of Anne Jones were laid out at the Auction Mart in Leicester on 27 May, 1929. Mr Eric Formby, a relative of Edward Hesketh Formby, kindly sent me the

The crowds surround the burial of Anne Jones.

catalogue for the sale. Among the items of furniture, the mementos and the bric-a-brac from Glandenys are mounted heads of horses, ladies' riding habits, pairs of ladies' riding boots and riding whips and crops. Poignant reminders of their owner's love of, if not obsession with, horses.

Anne Jones had made arrangements for the upkeep of the graves. She was anxious that they should be tended and properly cared for and had included a sum of money in her will for 'the upkeep of my little garden of rest at Tanybryn.' The sum of five pounds per annum was paid to local people to maintain the site and in 1967 a wire fence and a gate were erected to enclose the graves. Following Mrs Jones's burial, a tradition grew whereby local people would carry small white stones taken from the silver mine at Llanfair to place on the graves. Some of these little stones can still be seen to this day. Today, however, the graves are largely untended and are at the mercy of the elements and the encroaching undergrowth.

But all things pass. In the graveyard at Llanfair, William Jones's lonely grave was made of the finest, and most expensive, white marble surrounded by hand-wrought iron railings of a unique design. These

Cardiganshire and Carmarthenshire

Particulars and Conditions of Sale

OF THE VALUABLE FREEHOLD

RESIDENTIAL, AGRICULTURAL and SPORTING ESTATE

KNOWN AS THE

GLANDENYS ESTATE

extending to an area of approximately

3,719 acres

Which will be offered for SALE by PUBLIC AUCTION (except such Lots as may previously be disposed of by private treaty) at the

TOWN HALL, LAMPETER,

AT 1.30 P.M.

On FRIDAY, 2nd MAY, 1930,

BY

JOHN FRANCIS & SON

Particulars and Conditions of Sale, and any further information, may be obtained of

AUCTIONEERS—	SOLICITORS—
JOHN FRANCIS & SON,	Messrs. WALTERS & WILLIAMS,
CARMARTHEN.	CARMARTHEN.

have long been stripped away; on the discoloured stone, eroded by time and the weather, his name is now barely decipherable. Tanybryn, Formby's simple retreat where he and his lover could escape, is a forlorn heap of stones covered by crawling ivy and choked by the brambles. In 1930, the Glandenys estate, in the ownership of the Highmead family, was sold and the mansion was bought by Professor Cayo Evans of St. David's College, Lampeter and it is still owned by the family. Today, there is little to denote the site of the graves apart from two moss-covered mounds, a few scattered stones, a rusting gate and some vestiges of wire to keep out the curious sheep. Apart from the memories of a dwindling number of elderly inhabitants, not much is now known about them and their connection with this unique love story.

But this is also a tale of money, broken dreams, and ultimate betrayal. William Jones's aspirations for the Black Ox Bank were not to be realised. Had he lived he would have been saddened to see the institution he had so cherished ceasing to trade as an independent bank in 1909, and its connections with the family of David Jones the Drover coming to an end. His final years cannot have been comfortable ones. He had become a mere bystander as the relationship between his wife and Formby intensified. Today, Beddau'r Cariadon (The Lover's Graves), as they became known in the locality, still bear testimony to this tale of love and devotion. But one day they will also succumb to the neglect of the years. Anne Jones had specifically requested that there should be no mourning, no false piety and no tears at her funeral; the following lines resonate with her wishes and could well provide her with a fitting epitaph:

> Come not to mourn for me with solemn tread
> But laugh, as I have laughed with you . . .
> And be most merry – after I am dead.

> (Winifred Holtby: 1923.)

CHAPTER TWO

TREMBLE'S REVENGE

(The Broken Promise)

On Saturday morning, 19 August, 1876, a grim-faced horseman rode furiously along narrow lanes between Pumsaint and Llansawel. The sharp clatter of hooves suggested the urgency of his errand, for he was the bearer of appalling news. He had been sent from the mansion of Dolaucothi to fetch Dr Jenkins the surgeon, following a horrendous catalogue of events.

In his library Judge John Johnes, the squire of Dolaucothi, was slumped in a chair, bleeding profusely from gunshot wounds to his stomach. His daughter Charlotte lay unconscious on the kitchen floor, shot in the thigh and back. Even as the servant mercilessly whipped his horse, Henry Tremble, the butler was still intent on causing mayhem.

Dolaucothi, an attractive mansion situated on the banks of the river Cothi in the parish of Caeo near the village of Pumsaint, had long been the seat of the respected Johnes family. Pumsaint itself had since Roman times been a centre for gold mining, and the caves are still open to visitors today. But, it was not the lure of gold that prompted the tragic events of that day. Judge Johnes was one of the most cultured and respected figures in Wales. After graduating from Brasenose College, Oxford he became an accomplished lawyer and was appointed Recorder and Chairman of the Quarter Sessions for Carmarthenshire, but he was now long retired. Unlike many absentee landlords, Judge Johnes took a genuine interest in Welsh affairs. He was able to speak Welsh, the only language of most of his tenants, and had a reputation for treating them fairly. A man of culture, he attended the National Eisteddfod and entertained many English and Welsh luminaries at his mansion.

Dolaucothi mansion.

The intrepid traveller George Borrow came to Pumsaint in 1854 and in *Wild Wales* he describes a visit to Dolaucothi.

> After breakfast I departed for Llandovery. Presently I came to a lodge on the left hand side beside an ornamental gate at the bottom of an avenue leading seemingly to a gentleman's seat. On inquiring of a woman who sat at the door of the lodge, to whom the grounds belonged, she said to Mr. Johnes, and that if I pleased I was welcome to see them. I went in and advanced along the avenue which consisted

of noble oaks; on the right was a vale in which a beautiful brook was running north and south. I thought I had never seen a more pleasing sight . . . Presently, on the avenue making a slight turn, I saw the house, a plain but comfortable gentleman's seat with wings, 'With what satisfaction could I live in that house,' I said to myself, 'if backed by a couple of thousands a year'.

The Reverend Charles Williams, Principal of Jesus College, Oxford, a frequent visitor, described Dolaucothi as a 'place of wondrous serenity and imperturbable calm'. This calm was to be rudely shattered on that morning in August.

The perpetrator of these abominable events was Henry Tremble, a native of County Wexford in Ireland. Now aged thirty-six, he had been brought to Dolaucothi at the age of nineteen by the Judge's daughter, Charlotte. Her late husband, Captain Cookman, of Enniscorthy, had been particularly fond of Tremble and initially employed him as a stable boy. At Dolaucothi, where he proved to be a conscientious worker, he was promoted to gardener, gamekeeper and eventually to the prestigious post of butler to Judge Johnes. Now well settled at Dolaucothi, he married Martha, the daughter of a local farmer, and six children were born to them. By all accounts he was a good father, genuinely fond of his children, but his relationship with his wife deteriorated over the years as she became an alcoholic. By nature, however, Tremble was a loner with a brooding disposition. The strained situation at home added to his despair and was only made bearable by Susan, his eldest and favourite daughter who, although only fourteen, sought to look after the household.

Tremble's overriding ambition was to acquire the tenancy of the Dolaucothi Arms in Pumsaint, which was owned by Judge Johnes. Situated on the main road between Lampeter and Llandovery it was, in those days, much frequented by travellers. George Borrow stayed here on his journey and was much impressed by the hospitality provided.

I entered the inn of the 'Pump Saint'. It was a comfortable old fashioned place, with a very large kitchen and a rather small parlour. The people were kind and attentive, and soon set before me in the parlour a homely but savoury supper and a foaming tankard of ale.

After supper I went into the kitchen and sitting down with the good folks in an immense chimney corner, listened to them talking in their Carmarthenshire dialect till it was time to go to rest, when I was conducted to a large chamber where I found an excellent and clean bed awaiting me . . .

By all accounts, the tenancy had been promised to Tremble by the Judge as soon as the present licensee retired. When, in the summer of 1876, the inn became vacant, Tremble's hopes were naturally high. At the beginning of August he approached Judge Johnes, but to his astonishment and eventual fury, he was told that the tenancy was to be granted to John Davies, who was at the time the licensee of the Caio Inn. Why the Judge changed his mind is still not absolutely clear, but he could well have been influenced by the home circumstances of his devoted butler. An alcoholic wife would not have been a suitable partner for an aspiring innkeeper. Although Tremble was still favoured by Charlotte Cookman, the Judge had noted that his behaviour had deteriorated of late. He had become increasingly paranoid and frequently upset the other servants. When he confronted the Judge regarding the unfulfilled promise, bitter words flowed between them. These led to Tremble's dismissal from the post of butler with but one week's notice. There now raged within him an unquenchable desire for revenge against his former master. The sense of injustice that he felt grew and festered on his journey home as he contemplated what action he could take. On reaching his cottage, with his children in bed and his wife in a drunken stupor, he sat at the table to pen a letter addressed to the Reverend Charles Chidlow, Vicar of Caeo. His concern for his children is touching, but it is all too evident that he was now contemplating not only his his own end, but a course of action that would end in tragedy for others. He wrote:

> I Henry Tremble, Butler at Dolecothy do hereby authorise the Rev. Charles Chidlow, Cayo Vicarage, to take up my money that is now in the National Provincial Bank, Carmarthen, and to pay the said money quarterly to my Daughter Elizabeth Susan Tremble for the maintenance of herself and her sisters and brothers . . . I will leave all the money I can in a little box . . . the key of which I will enclose to you.

Sir, I hope you will excuse me taking this liberty, as I have no friends in this country nor do I know anyone that would be likely to take any interest in my children except you as a Christian clergyman. Hoping that at some future time you will be found amongst the good shepherds is the earnest wish of your obedient servant
Henry Tremble.
There will be about £8 in my pocket. H.T.

An extract from Henry Tremble's manuscript letter.

A small key was enclosed in a piece of blotting paper. No mention was made of Martha his wife.

Meanwhile, back at the mansion, the Johnes family were also oblivious of the depth of his resentment. His sacking had been an unpleasant affair for all concerned, but the Judge felt that he had been left with no alternative. He was relieved that the matter was at an end. Everything had now assumed an air of normality. Betha Johnes, the younger daughter, was visiting a dear friend, Lady Llanover, in Monmouthshire, while the Judge and Charlotte were entertaining Lady Wilkinson, the wife of Sir Gardiner Wilkinson, an eminent Egyptologist and archaeologist. She often stayed at the mansion to escape the hustle and bustle of London and, ironically as it turned out, always referred to it as her 'favourite sanctuary'. As a seasoned world traveller, she had many tales to tell, but by the time she departed from Dolaucothi on this occasion she would be able to recount the most distressing experience of her life.

On the surface, the morning of August 19 appeared normal, except that this was Tremble's last day in service at Dolaucothi. Margaret Davies, the cook was busy in the kitchen bottling the raspberry wine. Judge Johnes, whose health had been somewhat unpredictable of late, felt much better. He rose early and sat relaxing in the library reading *The Times* newspaper. Charlotte, eager to impress Lady Wilkinson, was doing the rounds with the servants ensuring that everything was ready for her guest. On passing the dining room, she noticed Tremble removing a silver tray presented to her father in 1861 following his resignation from the bench. Her suspicions were aroused and she ordered Tremble to replace the tray. She then asked him to place the rest of the silver on the table so that the various items could be counted before he left the mansion. A surly Tremble was obliged to obey. Although Charlotte had always looked with favour upon Tremble on account of her late husband, his summary dismissal by her father inevitably soured their relationship. Many months later she wrote in her Journal,

> This man, or rather fiend, had been a trusted servant in this house for seventeen years, and had lived besides with my husband from the time he was a boy helping in the stables . . . he never received anything but kindness from us all throughout.

In the meantime, Charlotte dismissed all thoughts of Tremble from her mind as she returned to the kitchen to ensure that the finest fare was provided for Lady Wilkinson. It was a busy day and everything had to be shipshape. No one took much notice of Tremble's sullen mood as he entered the room where the guns were kept. He was seen by Arthur Sturdy, a footman, who was to testify later that he had seen him loading a gun with powder and shot. Sturdy thought that he was going to shoot rabbits, but Tremble had other things on his mind. He made his way to the library where the Judge was still sitting, and within seconds the peace of the mansion was shattered by two deafening gunshots. Lady Wilkinson accompanied by Jane Jenkins, the maid, rushed to the library, where they were confronted with a most distressing sight. Judge Johnes was still sitting upright in his chair, but he was bleeding profusely from a gaping wound to the stomach. He was still calm and composed and was able to tell Lady Wilkinson, 'Tremble shot me. Mind he is taken.' Scarcely was she able to give the Judge what little comfort she could, before another couple of shots echoed menacingly from the kitchen. Despite being in great pain he urged her to 'see to Charlotte'.

By the time the now overwrought Lady Wilkinson reached the kitchen, she was met by another horrific sight. Two women lay insensible on the floor: Charlotte Cookman had been seriously wounded and Margaret her maid had fainted with shock. Charlotte later recalled the incident in her Journal.

> I heard a hurried step which made me turn round facing the door, where I saw Henry Tremble with a large breech loading gun in his hand take up his stand on the mat at the passage door, opposite the kitchen door. He raised the gun to his shoulder, took deliberate aim and said – 'Take that for your persecution of me.' – and fired at me. I saw the fire come out of the muzzle of the gun. I turned suddenly round and the whole charge entered my back and the fleshy part of my leg below the hip, the shots scattering over my back and down my thigh, I fell on my face towards the scullery door – the muzzle of the gun must have been about 7 or 8 feet from me, I think.

Meantime, the Judge was dying of his wounds in the library and seemingly beyond help. Under the supervision of Lady Wilkinson,

Charlotte was laid on a mattress and carried up to the Cotton Room to have her wounds poulticed. The whole mansion was now in a state of panic, confusion and fear. A terrified Anna Dixon, a maid, now encountered Tremble. He shouted out to her, 'I do not care for God, man or devil . . . If I thought she (Charlotte) was not dead, I'd beat her brains out with the butt of this gun.' Fortunately, she was spared, but he was now like a man possessed. He went out to the garden intent upon shooting Thomas the waggoner and Barney the gardener, but both men hid behind a shed. Consumed with hatred, he went for the dogs. Normally, he was fond of the dogs and used them for hunting, but now he was minded to destroy everyone and everything associated with Dolaucothi. He called the dogs out one by one and shot them in cold blood. This gruesome sight was witnessed by Thomas and Barney, but both were too frightened to intervene. When this act of wanton cruelty was completed, they witnessed Tremble setting out for Caeo, a man descending into a state of utter madness.

By the time Dr Jenkins reached Dolaucothi, it was too late to minister to the Judge. The doctor later testified:

> Mr. Johnes was sitting in a chair. On removing his clothes I noticed a large portion of the entrails protruding . . . It had a gunshot lacerated wound.

Fortunately, he was able to be of assistance to Charlotte, and over the coming months he treated her wounds. Following her recovery, she described her father's demise:

> My father died as he had lived. He died a saint with a blessing on his lips. His last words were 'God bless my children'. He never uttered a harsh word against his brutal murderer . . . he was the most virtuous, honourable man that ever lived, who was old and broken down, weakened by a long illness of two years' duration but, 'I will avenge saith the Lord'.

But what of Tremble, the perpetrator of the evil deeds at Dolaucothi? On reaching the village of Caeo, he sought out John Davies of the Caio Inn, the one appointed by Judge Johnes to be the licensee of the

1876

Dolau Cothy

Friday
Dec.ʳ
29"

Here there is a long and terrible
interval — On the morning of
the 19th of August last. I went
after breakfast to the Library
to see dear Papa as usual,
talked to him for a few minutes
chiefly about the Aneroid which
he had just bought & the difference
between it & the Barometer
Then I went out to the Kitchen
to order dinner — in passing
the Dining room door I saw
Henry Tremble the Butler
standing at the sideboard
reaching across as if to remove
the Silver Tray, (the one presented
to Papa on his resigning the
County Court Judgeship in 1861)
he was to leave his service
on that day by his own desire.

An extract from Charlotte Cookman's Journal.

Dolaucothi Arms, with the intention of shooting him as well. Fortunately, Davies was nowhere to be found. A witness to these events, John Williams, testified to the fact that he saw Tremble standing outside his house, Myrtle Villa, with a shotgun in his hand and a menacing look in his eyes. He told Williams, 'I have shot Mr. Johnes like a dog . . . I have done my duty . . . they thought they could tread upon my neck because I was an Irishman'.

On entering the house he tried to shoot his wife Martha, but she managed to deflect the gun and ran out taking her six terrified children with her. He then locked himself in an upstairs room and pointing his gun out of a window he threatened to shoot anyone who came too close.

By now two constables, PC Philip Morgan and PC Daniel Davies had arrived; a huge crowd had gathered and Myrtle Villa was under siege. News of the death of Judge Johnes and the circumstances surrounding it had spread like wildfire and the crowd was seething with rage and fear. The two constables tried to persuade Tremble to give himself up, but his only response was to point his gun and a pistol at the crowd. He then asked that his favourite daughter Susan, whom he called Bess, be allowed to bring him a glass of water. This request was granted, and for a while he embraced Susan before she emerged from the house in a very distressed state. Further efforts by the constables to get him to surrender peaceably were to no avail as he again appeared at the window. This time his thoughts were of Susan, and tears rolled down his cheeks as he called to the crowd below, 'If you can do anything for her, God bless you'. He disappeared from view and the crowd fell silent, then suddenly, the stillness was broken by a loud gunshot which echoed across the village. There was an audible gasp among the crowd accompanied by loud sobbing from Susan and the other children. His wife Martha fainted as the constables cautiously approached Myrtle Villa. They then entered the house and PC Morgan later described the scene that awaited them:

> I found Tremble on his back with the gun by his side . . . I also found a pistol on the table . . . He died in my presence fifteen minutes later.

This beautiful August day had witnessed a series of horrific events. A pillar of the community, a good and decent man, had been killed in his own library; his daughter had very nearly died as a result of gunshot wounds; now the author of these misfortunes lay dead on the floor of a cottage bedroom in the village of Caeo from a self-inflicted wound.

But this sad saga was far from over. There remained the need to dispose of the body of Henry Tremble, the deranged killer who had run amok and caused so much grief and horror within this tranquil west Wales community. Following the custom with regard to suicides, he would be buried at night without the benefit of a religious committal. The actual burial took place two days after his death. The Rev. Chidlow blessed his widow and children at the house; afterwards, the church wardens carried Tremble's coffin to the churchyard at Caeo. At 10.30pm on Monday, 21 August, in total silence and without ceremony, he was buried.

The death of Judge Johnes, however, prompted a sad response throughout Wales. At the National Eisteddfod held at Wrexham, the President asked the huge congregation to stand in order to pay their respects to 'that most talented and patriotic of Welshmen, Judge John Johnes of Dolaucothi.' He then addressed the crowd in sombre tones. This speech was recorded in *The Welshman,* August 1876.

> It is my duty, distressing as the circumstances are, to pay a tribute to one of the best sons of Cymru. (loud applause) . . . one who surely felt for the interests of his country, one who nobly fought in days gone by . . . That good man . . . beloved to every countryman. May I ask that this mighty assembly shall, in solemn, perfect, silence rise.

In sharp contrast to the hasty and clandestine interment of Tremble, the burial of the Judge was to be a public one, worthy of a man revered by all. Mourners assembled from all over Wales and their carriages extended over a distance of three miles from Pumsaint to Caeo. As Charlotte still lay seriously wounded in her room, only the hearse was allowed to proceed up the drive to the mansion lest she be disturbed. There was a distinct irony in the situation, for both the murderer and his victim were to be buried in the same churchyard – one to suffer the ignominy of burial in an unmarked grave in a remote corner, and the other to be laid to rest with dignity in the funeral vault of his ancestors.

The newspapers of the day gave full coverage to the funeral. A *Western Mail* reporter recorded:

> Nothing in my experience has impressed me so much as the melancholy proceedings today . . . A long dark stream of mourners, winding several miles through green lanes and meadows in bright glowing sunshine . . . the brave hearted heroism and devotion of a bereaved daughter . . . the tears and sorrowing faces of a multitude of neighbours and friends; the passing bell, the solemn service, the tender strains from the ancient church; the open tomb with the blackened coffins of generations of the Johnes family – and the launching of another coffin to add to the dark and silent resting place of his ancestors.

The funeral took place in the family vault and Miss Betha Johnes herself had picked a posy of wild white flowers to place on her father's coffin. A pall was thrown over the coffin bearing an inscription engraved on a massive brass shield.

John Johnes of Dolaucothi
Born April 6, 1800
Died August 19, 1876.

The burial service was conducted by the Reverend Canon Phillips in Welsh. Miss Betha Johnes, accompanied by Lady Llanover, placed a wreath on the coffin in the form of an inscription which read *Mewn Cof Annwyl*. She then kissed and placed upon the coffin her own posy of white flowers – taking it up and kissing it yet again before leaving it on the coffin. The only sound was the sobbing of the mourners. Thus, with

Judge John Johnes.

universal sadness and heartfelt tributes, the Judge's coffin was lowered to lie at peace with his ancestors.

But not so Tremble! There was no question of peace for his body. So abhorrent had been his deed in the eyes of the parishioners of Caeo that some of them could not bear the thought of a murderer lying in the same churchyard as his victim, the beloved Judge Johnes. Two months after his burial, they dug up his coffin and carried it to Llanddulas in Breconshire. There, they reburied it clandestinely in a pauper's grave. However, such a deed could not remain a secret for long, and when the villagers of Llanddulas became aware of the situation, they could not allow the body of Tremble to 'desecrate' their own churchyard. His coffin was dug up a second time and returned at night to Caeo. The wheels of the cart carrying him were bound with straw to muffle the noise. When the parishioners of Caeo woke the following morning, they found the coffin placed back in their own churchyard, with a note attached telling them to keep their own murderer. News of this macabre incident reached the ears of the Bishop of St David's. He strongly voiced his disapproval of the whole affair and wrote a trenchant letter to the parochial church councils at Caeo and Llanddulas:

> The following offences against Ecclesiastical Law have taken place.
>
> Viz.
>
> The removal of the body from Cayo Churchyard without a faculty.
> The interment in Llanddulas Churchyard without religious ceremony.
> The removal without authority from Llanddulas.
> The reinterment without authority at Cayo.
> I assure you the whole case has occasioned me a great pain and anxiety.
>
> W. Basil, St David's

Tremble was eventually reburied in an unmarked grave at Caeo Churchyard where he lies to this day.

Or does he? Some have maintained that he was moved yet again, but Mr William Dicks, who once lived in Tremble's house, maintained that:

> His body still lies in Caio Churchyard – underneath a coal shed built by the Dolaucothi family for the Church . . . The family wanted to obliterate all traces of the grave of the murderer.

But what of the surviving victims of this crime? Tremble's wife and his six children were inevitably scarred by this dreadful incident, although they were totally innocent parties. They could not have foreseen the depth of the resentment a hitherto loyal servant and loving father would harbour against the Dolaucothi family for a perceived wrong; a resentment that was to fester and mutate into a murderous intent. They could no longer bear the name of Tremble because of the ignominy now attaching to it. There was no option for them but to change their surname. As for the grievously injured Charlotte, she recovered after four months of careful nursing. In her journal she wrote 'I was in great danger, but it pleased God to raise me up again.' Her journal provides us with a unique record of the events that shattered the peace of Dolaucothi on that dreadful August day in 1876. She commenced it on 29 December of that same year with one purpose in mind:

> I write these lines that those who come after me, may read the true account of the awful tragedy which was enacted here on the 19th of August, 1876.

In this journal, she recounts her own version of the day's happenings including the nature of the threat posed to the family, a threat that should, on reflection, have been taken much more seriously. It also indicates that the shooting frenzy at Dolaucothi was a premeditated act of revenge planned beforehand by Tremble.

> Take note that the murderer was perfectly sane and not drunk or a habitual drunkard. The sole reason for these diabolical crimes was that Papa had – for many just and cogent reasons – refused him the Dolau Cothy Arms Inn at Pumpsaint . . . Betha my sister was thank God in London . . . but on the morning before she left Henry Tremble threatened us – 'Now yous (sic.) both together, I tell yous (sic.) that as sure as God's in heaven, yous (sic.) shall repent the injustice you have done to me.'

This journal is one of the few things that now remain to remind us of Dolaucothi and the illustrious family that once occupied it. Charlotte and Betha were so moved by the tributes paid to their father at the Wrexham

National Eisteddfod, that a letter was sent by Charlotte to the Reverend J. Griffiths, Rector of Neath, who had been called by the President to address the gathering and to ask 'this vast audience to signify its deep sympathy with that distressed family and the house which mourns the loss of one of the most loving sons of Wales.' The letter reads:

> Dear Canon Griffiths,
>
> I trust you will assure our countrymen, from my poor suffering sister and myself, that we, the daughters of the late John Johnes of Dolaucothy, offer our deep and heartfelt thanks to those who gave their solemn sympathy, and showed their sorrowful respect, for the memory of our beloved father in touching silence at the Wrexham Eisteddfod, on the 22d August. We shall never forget that testimony of his dear worth, who lived for truth, justice, and duty, and who died – although the death was bitter – with a blessing on his lips, and the peace of God within his heart. 'Gwyn ei fyd'. May we and all who love and honour his memory, meet him in the 'White World', amidst the 'Spirit of just men made perfect.' – Where the wicked cease from troubling, and the weary are at rest. –
>
> – C.A.M. Cookman (signed for her by her wish, by her sister)
> B. Johnes, Dolaucothy, 31st August, 1876.

Like Hafod, the magnificent mansion of Thomas Johnes, the Judge's earlier kinsman, Dolaucothi is no more. No longer in the ownership of the Johnes family, and having through neglect become unsafe, both suffered a similar fate. They were blown up by the Forestry Commission in the 1950s. The late Major Herbert Lloyd Johnes, a descendant of the Johnes family of Dolaucothi, added an interesting twist to the story of the mansion's destruction. He recalled that when it was being refurbished, he had set a carved stone from Maesyfelin, Lampeter, the mansion cursed by Vicar Prichard of Llandovery, into the wall of the library. Stones from Maesyfelin were also used by Sir Herbert Lloyd of Peterwell, when he improved his mansion in the eighteenth century. Today, not one of these mansions is left standing. Simply a coincidence, or does it hide something more sinister? As for the Dolaucothi Arms, it still survives as an inn. One wonders how many of those who call there for the odd drink have any idea of the catastrophe that the old tavern once precipitated.

Cefn Coch, the smallholding where Wil lived with his father in Llangwyryfon.

CHAPTER THREE

THE FUGITIVE

They sought him here
They sought him there,
But Lisburne failed
To find his lair.

This piece of doggerel composed by a local poet in 1868 describes the futile efforts of Edward Vaughan, Earl of Lisburne and the squire of Trawsgoed in Cardiganshire, to apprehend one William Richards, otherwise known as Wil Cefn Coch.

On a cold November evening the sound of a gunshot echoed sharply from Dolfor Wood in the parish of Llangwyryfon, which was part of the Trawsgoed estate. It was to have dramatic consequences that would lead to one of the most intensive manhunts ever seen in west Wales. It was the night of November 28, when William Richards of Cefn Coch and two brothers, Morgan and Henry Jones, Tŷnllwyn, set out to poach game on the land of Lord Lisburne. Times were hard for small peasant farmers; the common land had been enclosed, wages were low and the occasional hare, rabbit, or pheasant made a welcome addition to their meagre fare. Nevertheless, the gentry jealously guarded their game and held that the fish in the streams and the animals in the woods were theirs by a God-given right. Draconian game laws had been introduced to ensure that the common people respected this right. These were maintained on many estates by the imposition of mantraps and spring guns, although, strictly speaking, they had been illegal since 1827.

At Trawsgoed, five gamekeepers were employed to protect the game and to ensure that there was a plentiful supply available for the shooting parties invited by the Earl to visit his estate. The Head Keeper was Richard Jones, who undertook his role with relish, although the work could certainly have its dangers. It was claimed in the nineteenth century that the work of a gamekeeper was infinitely more dangerous than that of a soldier. Poachers who were caught could expect to suffer the full severity of the law. It could lead to a prison sentence and possibly transportation to the colonies for seven years. Faced with such a possibility, most poachers would not succumb easily, so gamekeepers had to be vigilant when forced to confront them. Nevertheless, the odds were clearly stacked against the poacher. It would only have been sufficient to catch a person in possession of a rod, a trap or a gun on private land to prove an intent to break the law and to secure a conviction.

The evening was cold but moonlit as Wil Cefn Coch and his companions threaded their way cautiously through the tangled undergrowth of Dolfor Woods. They knew the score, and were fully aware that they could not expect any mercy from Lord Lisburne if caught. To Wil, the very act of poaching was more than a means of providing a meal for the family; it was also an opportunity to challenge the autocratic rule of the gentry. There was no love lost between the tenant farmers in their cottages and the landlords in their mansions, and the pheasants and hares provided a nutritious alternative to their monotonous diet. Wil was a formidable, aggressive character, aged twenty-one, and standing five feet ten inches tall. He lived in Cefn Coch, a smallholding of thirteen acres at Llangwyryfon. Morgan Jones was twenty-three, but his young brother Henry was only fourteen. They lived in Tŷnllwyn, also in Llangwyryfon. Both he and Morgan Jones carried guns, and Henry Jones was armed with a stout stick. They carefully laid their snares and as there had been no sighting of the Trawsgoed keepers, Wil felt confident enough to dispatch two hares. It was a rash and foolish act, for on a clear and still night the gunshots reverberated throughout the woods. In fact, the gamekeepers were patrolling Tŷnberth Wood which was close by. The sound of the gun drew them hell for leather towards Dolfor, and soon the three poachers could hear the sound of footsteps crashing through the undergrowth crunching the bracken underfoot. Turning to flee, they realised that they could be trapped and caught. They made for the open fields with all the speed they could muster, but James Morgan, one of the keepers, had outflanked them. As the three reached Cwmbyr Cottage, he managed to grab and hold a by now petrified Morgan Jones. Although he struggled hard to release himself, he was held fast by the gamekeeper who was determined to hold on to his prisoner. In triumph, Morgan called out to Joseph Butler who was now fast approaching, 'Hooray Joe! Here they are!' Wil Cefn Coch and Henry Jones could only watch in horror as Morgan tried unsuccessfully to extricate himself, all the while shouting for help. James Morgan was unarmed, and when Wil trained his gun on him, called out in Welsh pleading with him not to fire, but he still held fast to Morgan Jones. Wil lowered his gun, but soon, they were conscious of Butler and the others approaching very quickly intent upon taking all three. Shades of the prison house were closing fast. More out of fear than with murderous intent, Wil raised his gun and, as Butler approached, fired. The blast caught Butler full in the sternum and he fell to the ground mortally wounded. At the inquest it was stated that the gun was less than twelve inches away from Butler's body when the shot was fired. In blind panic, Henry Jones and Wil took one look at the prostrate figure lying on the ground and ran wildly from the scene, leaving their companion Morgan Jones still in the custody of James Morgan. When questioned later by the police, he stated that the actual shot that killed Butler had been fired by William Richards of Cefn Coch. From that moment on, Wil Cefn Coch was a wanted man, and the hunt for him began immediately.

As it happened that evening, the thoughts of Edward Vaughan, the squire of Trawsgoed, were far removed from his pheasants and other game. November 28, 1868, was the day of a notable parliamentary election in Cardiganshire. Vaughan had stood as the Tory candidate, and since the Trawsgoed family had treated the county as its fiefdom over many years, he had been confident that he would keep his seat. This time, however, the franchise had been extended, and many working-class males had been given a vote for the first time. Because secret ballots were not introduced until 1872, tenants still had to declare their political allegiances in full view of their landlords. To vote contrary to the landlord's directions took a great deal of courage, but this time many chose to do so. For their temerity, a number were cruelly evicted from their holdings, but they had ensured that the Tory hegemony had been broken once and for all. It had been a hard-fought election and a bruising contest in a literal sense. One hundred special constables, armed with staves and paid five shillings, had to be sworn in to keep the peace in Aberystwyth. In spite of this, Vaughan's valet had been beaten up on the street and forced to seek refuge in the Cambrian Vaults. The windows of his election agent in Pier Street had been broken by a mob, and gangs of urchins had pelted his supporters with mud. One Tory who had the temerity to shout 'Vaughan for ever' had his face kicked in and his left thumb almost bitten off. To add insult to injury, the unthinkable had happened! For the first time ever the Vaughans of Trawsgoed had been defeated by a Liberal candidate. Already, he was in a foul, vindictive mood, but more was to come. Sorrows, after all, come in battalions!

Incensed by his defeat, Vaughan was now informed that his keeper, Joseph Butler, had been shot by a poacher and lay dead near Cwmbyr Cottage. With the identity of his killer already widely known, a furious Vaughan was determined to see him brought to justice swiftly. He immediately offered a substantial reward of £100 for information leading to the arrest and conviction of one William Richards, otherwise known as Wil Cefn Coch. For a community living constantly on the verge of destitution, such a vast sum must have proved very tempting. Morgan Jones was held in custody at Llanilar, and within a day, his frightened brother Henry gave himself up. But the real prize was still at large. Members of the Cardiganshire Constabulary converged on the Trawsgoed and Mynydd Bach area like vultures, and it seemed only a matter of time before Wil would be apprehended.

But as the days progressed, there was still no sign of Wil Cefn Coch in spite of the massive efforts to bring him to justice. He had gone to earth, and, surprisingly, no one had come forward with information leading to his capture in order to claim the reward. It appeared that the community was closing ranks, in order to protect one of their own, albeit one who was accused of murder, and one who would, most certainly, face the gallows if captured. Some of the more radical members of the community were determined that the by-now desperate Wil should not fall into the hands of the police. They did not view Wil

£100 REWARD

WHEREAS on the night of FRIDAY, the 27th of NOVEMBER instant, JOSEPH BUTLER, Keeper to the Right Honourable The Earl of Lisburne, was Shot dead by WILLIAM RICHARDS, of Cefncoch, in the Parish of Llangwryddon, in the County of Cardigan; the above Reward will be paid for the apprehension of the said William Richards.

The said William Richards is about 28 years of age, 5ft. 9in. or 10in. high, slight figure, long thin legs, with stooping gait, light hair slightly curled, thin sandy whiskers, long thin face, lower teeth overlapping upper teeth, long nose rather Roman, full grey eyes, speaks very little English; is supposed to be dressed in a dark home-made coarse coat, corduroy breeches and leggings, striped check shirt, and lace-up boots, clumsy feet, and has been operated upon for a bruise in the testicle.

All information to be addressed to the Superintendent of Police at Aberystwith.

Crosswood, 30th November, 1868.

J. COX, PRINTER AND STATIONER, PIER STREET, ABERYSTWITH.

£100 Reward for the capture of Wil Cefn Coch.

as an ordinary criminal, but as one who embodied the struggle between the peasantry and their masters. Among the most notable of his defenders was Dafydd Thomas Joseph, a clock mender from Trefenter, a man who held fast to his radical principles. With policemen combing every inch of the terrain in and around Trawsgoed, keeping Wil hidden required a great deal of initiative, subterfuge and above all a tremendous amount of luck. On the other hand, the resolve of the gentry to secure the conviction of one who was regarded by them as nothing more than a common murderer added to the pressure placed upon the police to capture him.

Posters were published and distributed throughout the county giving a detailed description of Wil Cefn Coch. It was hardly a flattering one. He is described as having 'long thin legs and a stooping gait . . . thin sandy whiskers . . . a long thin face . . . lower teeth overlapping upper teeth . . . and clumsy feet'. Not the appearance of a Ned Kelly, or a conventional folk hero! The poster also contains one embarrassing detail. It indicates that Wil had been 'operated upon for a bruise on his testicle'. Within days of the appearance of the poster, the police were searching barns, cottages and farm outhouses around Trefenter and Mynydd Bach. No stone was to be left unturned in their efforts to flush out the fugitive. But as the days wore on, they were no nearer to catching Wil; it seemed he had simply disappeared into thin air.

Constantly on the move, he was passed around from one place to another. He was conveyed in his cart by the wily Joseph, who hid him in a long case clock as he plied his trade throughout the area. There were many narrow misses as Wil came perilously close to capture. On one occasion a suspicious sergeant decided to search a certain cottage. Dafydd Joseph got wind of his intention, and Wil had to conceal himself under the bedclothes of a woman who had just given birth to a child. He had to remain motionless while the sergeant searched the bedroom. Distracted by the noise of a screaming newborn infant, the policeman was forced to depart empty-handed. On another occasion, while staying with a miller, he had to hide in the revolving machinery of the mill while the flour was being ground. When the miller was asked by the police to stop the machinery so that they could search the mill race, he agreed to do so on condition that they paid for the resultant loss of production. The constables thought better of it, and concluding that no living person could survive among the revolving cogs and wheels, they went on their way.

Meanwhile, the weeks grew into months and the frustration of Edward Vaughan and his fellow gentry became increasingly evident. With such a substantial reward on offer, it had been assumed that by now the temptation would have been too much for someone in the locality. The Superintendent of Police was under tremendous pressure, but all his efforts to date had been to no avail, for Wil was still free. Stung by the criticism from the gentry, he ordered that more and more posters be displayed throughout Cardiganshire and beyond. Surely, someone somewhere would take the bait, but no one did.

Even so, Wil's life was becoming unbearably difficult. Always on the move, always looking over his shoulder, both he and his protectors appreciated that this tense situation could not continue. He had been hidden in chapel vestries, barns, hayricks, chimneys, outhouses, and on occasions he had to brave the elements and hide out of doors in the woods and the remote acres of Mynydd Bach. At the same time the temptation of the £100 was hanging constantly over his head. More threatening still, it was believed that the members of one family in particular were seriously contemplating the reward. On the other hand, those who were protecting him were compromising their own safety; there was no alternative other than to get him out of the country – but how? All the roads were being closely watched, as was the coast around the harbour at Aberaeron. But help was at hand from an unexpected quarter.

pic. Gerald Morgan

Joseph Butler's Grave.

John 'Ivon' Jones was a prominent figure in the business and cultural life of Aberystwyth. He was a grocer, an ardent chapel-goer and had served as secretary of the National Eisteddfod held in the town in 1865. On the surface, he was hardly the kind of person who would wish to be embroiled in the events surrounding the shooting of a gamekeeper. But he had a radical streak. He despised the rule of the gentry and what he perceived to be their oppression of the poor. It was no accident that his grandson, also Ivon Jones, was later credited with founding the Communist Party in South Africa. Like many within Cardiganshire, he regarded Wil Cefn Coch as a folk hero, and was prepared to assist in spiriting him out of the country. But where to? During the nineteenth century, thousands had emigrated from the county in the search for a better life overseas. The majority had gone to America, and the most favoured states were Ohio and Wisconsin. By the middle of the century there were well-established Welsh communities in the state of Ohio, and such was the predominance of immigrants from the villages of central Cardiganshire in the counties of Jackson and Gallia that the region was known as the 'Cardiganshire of America.' The area was dotted with farmsteads bearing such names as Lledrod, Cilcennin, Caerwedros, Abermeurig and Blaenpennal. This seemed the ideal place to shelter a fugitive like Wil, for he would be among his own kinfolk and could expect some assistance and protection. The port of Liverpool was the main departure point for emigration to America. It would be an extremely difficult task to get him there from west Wales, for his description had been distributed far and wide, and the police were targeting ports in particular. John Ivon Jones, assisted by the ever faithful Dafydd Joseph of Trefenter, had mapped out a route which would seek to avoid the police roadblocks. Disguised as a woman, in a voluminous dress and wearing a large hat to hide his face, Wil was provided by Ivon Jones with a sum of money so that he could start a new life across the Atlantic. Keeping to mountain tracks and avoiding centres of population whenever possible, Dafydd and Wil succeeded in outwitting the police.

At last they reached Liverpool and made their way to the port which was crowded with emigrants waiting to board the ships. Nevertheless, they felt extremely vulnerable when they saw the wanted posters of Wil and details of the reward emblazoned all over the docks. Even so, they managed to keep their cool and to blend in with the mass of people, many of whom were Welsh, crowding the dock. Tensions were high as the would-be emigrants took leave of their distressed relatives; in many cases forever. Dafydd bought a ticket and, in the midst of scenes of heightened emotion, Wil sought to mingle with the other passengers boarding the ship unchallenged. Edward Morgan of Venezuela, who wrote about the affair later, suggested that policemen actually boarded the ship at the last moment to look for Wil, but failed to find him. After hours of unbearable tension, the vessel at long last weighed anchor and set sail for the New World with Wil on board. According to Edward Morgan again, as the ship disappeared from view, Dafydd Joseph, overcome with emotion sank to his knees crying out 'Diolch i Dduw, 'rwyt ti'n saff o'r diwedd!' ('Thank God you are safe at last!'). Over the past few months he and others had risked all. Had their complicity in the affair been detected, they would most certainly have been convicted and sentenced to long terms of imprisonment.

Meanwhile, back in Cardiganshire the hunt continued, for Lord Lisburne was still intent upon bringing to justice the man who had so callously shot his keeper. Eventually, however, it dawned upon the authorities that Wil had escaped the net and was now beyond their reach. There is an uncorroborated story that an officer was chosen to cross over to America to apprehend Wil in order to bring him back to face the full rigour of the criminal law. Somehow or other, Wil got to know of this and wrote to the officer concerned warning him that should he ever venture to America he would not return alive, as there were enough tall trees there to hang him. Apparently, this threat had the desired effect, as the officer thought better of the venture and heeded Wil's warning. Therefore, much to the chagrin of Lord Lisburne and the embarrassment of the police, who had devoted huge resources to capture him, the hunt was discontinued.

They now had to content themselves with the fact that Morgan Jones, one of the accomplices, had been apprehended due to the courage of the keeper James Morgan. Although he had been armed, he had not actually fired a shot, nevertheless, he was charged before the Llanilar Magistrates of being an accessory to the murder of Butler, together with the offence of poaching. Due to the seriousness of the allegations, he was remanded in custody to face trial at the next Assizes. His brother was also brought into court in handcuffs after confessing to being the third poacher and giving himself up to the police. He was also remanded in custody. When Morgan Jones eventually appeared at the Cardiganshire Assizes in March 1869, his defence claimed that he had not participated in the shooting of Butler and, as he was being held by James Morgan when the shot was fired, he was technically in custody at the time so that he could not have been an accessory. The Judge agreed, and Jones was only tried for the lesser offence of poaching. Surprisingly, he got off with the comparatively light sentence of one year's imprisonment with hard labour. There is no record of his brother Henry ever being brought to trial as the police never managed to draw up a conclusive case against him.

We have no knowledge of Wil Cefn Coch's voyage out, but in the Spring of 1869, he reached the sanctuary of the United States. Mr Evan Davis of Oak Hill has provided a valuable account of Wil's life in America based on the recollections of those in the community who knew him. Two farmers, who had previously been his neighbours in Wales, arranged for him to be collected in Altoona, Pensylvania and brought to Ohio. Over five thousand people had left Cardiganshire to settle in America in the nineteenth century. For them it was an escape from the grinding poverty at home and in the 'promised land' they hoped that new opportunities would await them. In his *Industrial History of Oak Hill, Ohio,* Evan Davies refers to the contribution made by the Welsh who brought with them their language and culture. Wherever they had gone, they had established their square, plain chapels and their log-cabin schools which became the hub of the social, religious and educational life of the newly established communities. These were dotted around parts of Ohio providing an essential link between the newcomers and the land they had left. Not all the emigrants made good; many had to endure a life of hard labour and abject poverty while others became prosperous business and industrial entrepreneurs. Evan Davis adds, however, that

> These early Welsh were not all temperate; some of them were heavy drinkers. Indeed, there were a few 'defaid du' ('black sheep') among them who were fugitives from justice.

Wil was among these.

He was taken to the small settlement of Horeb, which lay two-and-a-half miles west of the township of Oak Hill in Jackson County, Ohio. The first group of Welsh immigrants had arrived here in 1818 from Cilcennin in Cardiganshire. Thereafter, there was a constant flow. A number met in the Ship Inn, Pennant, and decided to emigrate to Ohio as a group. As well as clearing the virgin forests and preparing the land for farming, some became pioneers of industry. Horeb and Oak Hill were centres for the brick and iron industries and natives of Cardiganshire were influential in setting up the Cambria and Jefferson furnaces and the Oak Hill Fire Brick and Coal company. Here Wil would be among his own kind, but it would still require a strenuous effort on his part to put the events of the past months behind him and to adapt himself to a completely different way of life.

In order to gain entry into the United States, Wil had changed his name to Evan Morgan. According to Evan Davis, his initial behaviour did not endear him to the 'respectable' elements in the Welsh community. Here he was not accorded the hero status that had enabled him to escape from Cardiganshire, and was 'feared, disliked and considered a disgrace' by many. At first, he found employment as a farm labourer travelling from farm to farm. Finding it hard to settle down in his new environment, he became prone to bouts of heavy drinking which often led to violent displays of temper. He was given work by a Mrs Jane Lloyd, a widow, who also employed an Irish maid. The maid took a sadistic pleasure in taunting Wil about his very limited command of English. One Saturday night, he returned after a session of heavy drinking, and on being goaded by the maid, he completely lost his temper. He grabbed a butcher's knife and lunged at her. Fortunately, he missed, but after severing part of her dress, the knife became embedded in a cupboard. Others present sought to restrain him, but this violent outburst had frightened his employer and he was sacked. Fortunately, no further action was taken as the conduct of the maid was deemed to be provocative, but those within the community had now become aware of another side to his character, which was not a very pleasant one. Nevertheless, he soon managed to find employment with the Jefferson Iron Company, where the majority of the workforce was Irish, many of whom were hard drinkers like himself. Because he had earned an unenviable reputation for violence, the Town Marshall kept an eagle eye on him and he was constantly warned of the perils of strong drink.

Fortunately, in 1872, his world was set to change as the story takes a romantic turn. Wil had been courting Elizabeth Morgan from Pontryhydfendigaid back in Wales, and she decided to join him in America. She was twenty-six years of age and was, by all accounts, a very sensible person with a sunny disposition. She had worked for two years in London in order to earn money for the passage. In spite of the events of the past four years, she had retained her affection for Wil. One of her brothers had already emigrated to Ohio some years previously, and she was now accompanied by another two. They cannot have been entirely happy about the possibility of a reunion between their sister and a rather wild and unruly character prone to violence and drunkenness. Elizabeth, however, was confident that she could tame Wil Cefn Coch and keep his violent moods in check. She did indeed prove to be a calming influence throughout his life. Constantly looking over his shoulder, Wil had changed his name yet again. He was now to be known as David D. Evans. Within a year of her arrival in Horeb, Wil and Elizabeth were married and they set up home in a small log cabin owned by the Jefferson Furnace Company. A few years later they purchased a small farm about two miles south of Oak Hill. Elizabeth became a respected member of the local chapel and was highly regarded in the community for her good works. Evan Davis remarked that the influence of religion was responsible for sustaining Welsh culture in these early settlements. The chapel influence meant that gambling, horse racing, drinking, and Sunday amusements were frowned upon. This Calvinistic narrowness was referred to as the 'Welsh menace' by those of other nationalities who lived in these predominantly Welsh communities.

Wil preferred to remain on the fringes of society and never accompanied his wife on a Sunday to chapel. He did seek to advance his business prospects, for in addition to farming, he set himself up as a coal merchant. No children were born to them, but they did adopt an orphan boy named Henry Pettit who grew up to be a well-respected citizen. His descendants still live in the locality. Wil proved to be a good father to his adopted son, but increasingly he became an isolate, rarely leaving the farm except to deliver coal.

The shades of the past seemed to cast a continual shadow over his life. It is said that he always slept with a loaded revolver under his pillow. His wife's family had prospered in the community; one of her nephews became the manager of the Oak Hill Fire Company while another established a large fire-clay business. They also played a prominent role in local politics, but they always found it difficult to accept that Elizabeth had married Wil Cefn Coch. By 1921, he had spent fifty-two years exiled from Wales. He was fortunate that he had been able to spend them within a Welsh community where he could express himself daily in his mother tongue. He had also been fortunate in his marriage, but most of all he could count himself lucky that he had escaped the dire consequences of that act of folly committed on a moonlit November night in Dolfor Woods so many years ago. By now his health was failing and, possibly conscious that life was ebbing away, he joined the Oak Hill Welsh Congregational Chapel. Was this his final act of atonement? Two weeks later, in February 1921, he died peacefully in his bed at the age of seventy-six and was buried in Oak Hill cemetery. He appears to have outlived his legend, for his obituary in the *Oak Hill Press* of 10 February merely notes that,

> David D. Evans passed away at his home about two miles south of town, Monday evening. Mr. Evans was 76 years of age. He was born in Wales and while young emigrated to this country. He is survived by his wife Elizabeth Evans. Funeral service will be held at the Congregational Chapel, Friday, at 9.30 a.m.

There is no mention of the turbulent episode that had brought him to Ohio all those years ago. Elizabeth survived her husband, and lived to the grand old age of ninety. She was buried alongside him in the Morgan family section of the Calvinistic Methodist Cemetery in Oak Hill. Her obituary in the *Oak Hill Press* refers to the fact that she came to America with her brothers Evan and Dan Morgan, her brother James having preceded them. Her parents and her other brother William eventually followed, leaving her sister Ann as the only family member remaining in Wales. The Morgan family prospered in Oak Hill. They were very well regarded in the community and became active in local

The respectable gravestone of Wil and his wife as it stands today in Oak Hill.

pic. Bet Davis, Maesglas, Ohio

politics. Wil, however, remained the 'black sheep' within the family, and was, according to Evan Davis, 'a problem they did not like to discuss.' Elizabeth Evans's obituary testified to the prominent role she had always played in the religious life of Oak Hill. Although many continued to regard Wil as 'her burden', she was given a great deal of credit within the community 'for reforming him' and for reining in the unpleasant aspects of his character.

Far from Ohio, there is another gravestone which continues to remind us of the escapades of Wil Cefn Coch. It stands in the churchyard of Llanafan in Ceredigion, and it has on it the name of Joseph Butler. Underneath his name is carved the stark inscription, *Shot by a poacher.*

CHAPTER FOUR

CHARLATANS OR HEALERS?

Blow on a dead man's embers
And a live flame will start.
(Robert Graves)

Although long dead, the fame of Dr John Harries and his son Henry has never really been extinguished. Go to the Cothi Valley in Carmarthenshire and the older generation will eagerly regale you with weird tales of strange rituals which occurred here in the nineteenth century. Still engrained in folk memory are accounts of the people who flocked to Pantcoy, the home of Dr Harries of Cwrtycadno, in search of cures for all manner of afflictions. The old beliefs lingered on long after his death in 1839 and these were passed down from generation to generation. In country areas, superstition dies hard.

John Harries was born in 1785 at Pantcoy and subsequently achieved fame and much notoriety as a '*Dyn Hysbys*' or a 'Cunning Man.' The folklorist Marie Trevelyan writing at the turn of the last century called him 'the most remarkable renowned man in the South, popularly known as the Dyn Hysbys and capable of manifestations.' Persons who possessed such gifts were sometimes called 'wizards' or 'conjurers' and could belong to two categories. Malicious conjurers were deemed to have sold themselves to the devil in return for their powers, while the more benign gained their magical arts from the study of secret books and used their talents to thwart the designs of evil forces. Harris belonged to the latter category, not that he would have accepted the term 'conjurer' as applying to himself. He always referred to himself as a 'surgeon', but the true extent of his medical qualifications has long been a matter of conjecture.

During the eighteenth and early nineteenth centuries the medical profession was divided into three categories. The most prestigious practitioners were the physicians; armed with medical degrees, they claimed to belong to a learned profession. Then came the surgeons whose training was largely by apprenticeship supplemented by attendance at some medical classes. Thirdly, there were the apothecaries who were the pharmacists of their day. Surgeons were mainly responsible for routine medical tasks such as setting bones, blood letting, lancing boils, ministering to diseases of the skin, venereal disease and inoculating against smallpox. This proved to be a common and lucrative practice following Edward Jenner's discovery in 1798 that inoculation with cowpox was effective. In rural areas it was sometimes necessary for a

Pantcoy, 1984. A new building replaced the original home of Dr Harries to the left.

pic. Geraint Phillips

surgeon to combine his role with that of an apothecary in order to provide both the treatment and the essential medicines required by patients.

Mrs Ithiel Vaughan Poppy, a descendant, provided a family history now kept in the National Library of Wales. She recounts conversations with her grandfather David Vaughan-Harries, who visited Pantcoy as a child and was present at Dr Harries's funeral. John Harries always referred to himself as 'surgeon' and it is claimed that at the age of eighteen he attended Oxford University and then the Royal College of Surgeons in Scotland qualifying as an M.R.C.S. and an M.D. It has also been claimed that he set up a surgery in Harley Street before returning to the less august surroundings of rural Carmarthenshire. There is proof, however, that he was trusted by the inhabitants of west Wales and beyond, to minister to their medical needs in a conventional sense, but that he was also to be regarded as a provider of unconventional cures after communing with supernatural forces. It is this supposed ability that gave him a certain fame but also a degree of notoriety. By all accounts he was an imposing figure, over six feet tall and well built. His formidable appearance was enhanced by the long heavy velvet cape lined with red Welsh flannel that he always wore, adding to the sense of awe that he engendered among the more superstitious of those seeking his assistance.

At a time when people felt helpless in the face of so many endemic diseases, Harries was reputed to have a cure for most. His abilities encompassed ailments of the body as well as conditions of the mind. His practice flourished, and his account book reveals that he treated a large number of patients every month. With no where else to turn, people trudged to Pantcoy to seek relief from their troubles. Pantcoy is an isolated and sequestered farmhouse high above the Cothi Valley, sheltered from the winds by a rocky outcrop to the rear of the house. In Dr Harries's day, it was served by a well-trodden track, and even today the route which leads from Cil-y-cwm to Cwrtycadno is known by some of the locals as Llwybr yr Hen Ddoctor Harries ('the Old Dr Harries's Way').

Dr Harries kept meticulous details of his patients, their illnesses, and the medication prescribed. His prescription book also contains details of over five hundred prescriptions most of them prepared by him at

Pantcoy. The cost of the medication and the expenses claimed by him when he travelled far afield are carefully noted in his day book. This shows him wandering from farm to farm seeking to cure all manner of afflictions. The following are a few extracts from this book.

> Rachel Davies, Llwyncelyn, attendance to dislocation, embrocation cost 9\6d, for lancing thumb and dressing cost 1s\1d . . . Samuel Davies, Caegwyn, aperient for children, cost 3d . . . David Smith, Lampeter, reduce dislocation in shoulder cost 7s\6d . . . George Lewis, Dolecothy, dressing cut, cost 4d . . . Sally Williams, Dolecothy, dressing cut on leg, cost 3d . . . For child at Tregaron, Calomel, cost 4d . . . David Thomas, Pentwyn, Flor. Sulphor cost 8d . . . Thomas Jones, Weaver, Mist. Diaphor cost 3s\6d, Emroc. and dressing finger 2s.

Harries also treated children with cowpox to protect them from the scourge of smallpox. John Clunwy of Rhandir paid five shillings for his children to be vaccinated. Poor David Rees, Blaengwiail, had a problem with his scrotum and paid two shillings and thruppence for a cure. John Jones, of Brynambor on the mountain above Llanddewibrefi, was charged three shillings and sixpence for bleeding. Sick farm animals were also treated, and John Harry Smith, Erwlwyd, paid three pence for embrocation oil for horses and three pence to cure a sick cow.

Dr John Harries was a familiar figure on the roads as he visited one farm after another attending to the sick. Sometimes he would travel on horseback, his saddlebags bulging with an assortment of medicines. At other times a pony and trap would be more appropriate to carry the surgical instruments, the collection of leeches, the bowls for blood-letting and the glass vessels for cupping, when heated cups were held against the flesh to draw poisonous elements from the body. The response of those who greeted him as he passed by was one of respect mingled with an element of fear. His practice covered a wide area and his ministrations were not only sought by the peasant farmers but also by the local gentry. There are frequent references to the visits paid by him to Dolaucothi, the mansion of the Johnes family at Pumsaint. In July and August, 1824, he was called by Mrs Johnes on no less than nine occasions to attend to her four-year-old daughter Charlotte, who was sick. Similarly, he attended at Briwnant to provide cowpox injections for all the children.

The Doctor required prompt payment for his services as testified by this invoice sent to his patients:

To Medicine and Medical attendance
As per account rendered . . . £

Sir,
Unless the above amount be paid to me on or before the — day of — — next, adverse means will be resorted to, for the recovery.

Your humble servant,
John Harries

The nature of the 'adverse means' is not altogether clear, but with the Doctor's ability to instil fear in his patients, it is highly unlikely that they would wish to find out.

As his fame spread, so did the requests from patients living further afield. On 15 February 1829, one Philip Lawler rode all the way from Clydach Iron Works to seek a cure for his wife and was charged five shillings. John Harries and his son Henry, who now assisted him, had at their disposal a well-stocked dispensary. It was claimed that they had tinctures for treating most ailments. These were mainly herbal; they made use of digitalis, hartshorn, comfrey, meadowsweet, willow bark, dock root, rosemary, lavender, and they also made extensive use of sulphur. Leeches were commonly used for bleeding and for cleaning infected wounds, while purgatives for cleansing the gut were greatly in demand. Not all the medication dispensed by the Doctor led to a successful outcome, as he himself readily confessed in his day book. In 1820, he had prescribed a specific cure for one Elin Morgan, but he had to admit that it had availed her nought. 'I am informed that she was dead. Medicine prepared useless.'

The treatment afforded by Dr Harries for the mentally ill was, to say the very least, unconventional, if not downright gruesome. At this time there was very little understanding of mental illness; methods of dealing with it often bordered upon the cruel, as patients were confined to the so-called asylums. Apparently, the Doctor had devised his own unorthodox cure for those unfortunate mental patients brought to him for treatment. Accompanied by his friend, Theophilus the blacksmith, he would take the patient to a deep pool in the river Cothi. He would then draw a pistol and, without warning, fire it close to the ear of the poor patient, who, scared out of his or her wits, would jump into the pool. The patient would then be saved from drowning by the blacksmith and brought to the river bank. We have no records to show the success or otherwise of such a drastic method. However, the belief persisted locally that it worked, possibly because of the sudden fright and the shock of the immersion in cold water.

On another occasion, the relatives of a severely depressed boy went to Pantcoy for help. The Doctor concluded that his condition was due to a fear of water and he offered to cure the boy. This treatment was even more outlandish than usual. He sent his son, Henry, to catch a frog in the stream running alongside the house, but told him to keep it well hidden. After examining the boy, he informed him that he had swallowed a tadpole which had now grown into a frog, and that this was the cause of all his problems. The patient was naturally alarmed, but Harries assured him that he could be treated. He was given an emetic which made him violently sick. The hidden frog was then produced and the boy told that he had vomited it and would now be cured. The patient was then sent on his way mightily relieved and in a state of some euphoria. We will never know whether or not this bizarre treatment provided a permanent cure for his depression!

Tuberculosis was endemic in many rural communities in west Wales at this time, and led to the early deaths of young people in particular. Dr Harries, like his contemporaries, had no cure for this, however. In 1832, a cholera epidemic raged through the land unchecked, but when Harries could not cure his patients he attributed the cause of death to a visitation from God. There were 102 deaths in Carmarthen alone, and Methodist preachers like John Elias delivered fiery sermons striking fear among their congregations with threats of impending doom and the dangers of hell. For other complaints, Harries had an impressive armoury of cures. He could, apparently, provide forty-five scripts for gonorrhoea. Deaths in childbirth were all too frequent at this time and for puerperal fever he prescribed cinnamon. For dysentery in children he provided a tincture of digitalis. Many of the plants used were grown in specially cultivated soil by a gardener who was employed by the Doctor.

But Harries's reputation rested mainly on the widespread belief that he possessed supernatural powers. In the years following his death many anecdotes relating to these supposed powers were passed from generation to generation in the Cothi valley. As folk tales are told and retold, they are embellished and almost certainly exaggerated, but quite often at their core there may well be a grain of truth. Such tales are very much alive in the memories of the older generation. Although their veracity may be questioned in our more sophisticated age, they give us a glimpse of the way the Doctor was perceived within his community. He mixed medicine with magic, claiming the powers of a seer, a clairvoyant, a wizard and a 'cunning man' as well as the skills of a physician. Typical of these stories is the one relating to the disappearance of a girl from Tregaron. In spite of strenuous searches she could not be found, so her distraught parents turned to Harries for help. He was able to tell them that their daughter's body lay beside a brook and beneath a tree in whose hollow trunk there was a wild bees' nest. He could also tell them that she had been murdered by her sweetheart. Following these instructions the body was found and eventually her lover confessed to the crime.

In July, 1825, another murder took place in the vicinity of a farm called Llwynfynwent in the parish of Newchurch. He was again called upon, this time to find the body of Peggy Williams of Ffrydiau. He pointed to a shallow grave near to some marshy ground close to the farm. According to the report presented to the Breconshire Great Sessions, the body was discovered 'in some wet land like a bog . . . after the people had been digging for a short time . . . she was clothed in a gown, petticoat and shift.' She had been strangled and was pregnant; once again her lover was a suspect and he eventually confessed to the crime. This time, however, Harries found himself in hot water as the magistrates, Sackville Gwynne of Glanbran and Lloyd of Glansevin, took a more sceptical view of his powers. They felt that his knowledge of the body's whereabouts must have made him an accessory to the crime, as they could not accept that he was the possessor of supernatural powers. Determined to prove that he had such powers, he challenged each of them to put their dates of birth on slips of paper, and he would then be able give them the actual dates of their own deaths. Not one of them took up the challenge and Harries was exonerated and allowed to leave the court.

Thomas Davies of Pencarreg related a story told by his mother concerning an event reputed to have taken place near Gwernogle. This again concerns Dr Harries's ability to discover the whereabouts of bodies. A farm labourer named Morgan worked on the local farms, but one winter he disappeared, and strenuous efforts to find him proved futile. One day a sheepdog was seen with a bone in its mouth at Crynarth farm, but it was such an unusual looking bone that no one could suggest where it came from. Eventually, it was shown to be a human bone. In spite of searches in the vicinity of the farm, no further evidence was found although it was suspected that it had a bearing on the disappearance of Morgan. Someone suggested that the assistance of Dr Harries should be sought. After an argument, many villagers expressed the view that this was superstitious nonsense and a waste of time. Nevertheless, those who had suggested this course of action travelled the fifteen miles to Pantcoy. After listening intently, Harries told them that what remained of the body could be found in some woods near a craftsman's house. Near Crynarth was a woodturner's cottage close to some woods. Following a detailed search of the woods, a skeleton was discovered, together with a pair of boots and a pocket knife. This was recognised as Morgan's. The remains were buried in the churchyard at Llanfihangel Rhos-y-Corn, and Thomas Davies maintained that the spot where the body was found became known locally as Gwâl Morgan (Morgan's Lair).

In 1838, a young man from Pembrokeshire who had been confined to his bed for months with no apparent illness or disease was brought by his desperate family to Pantcoy. The Doctor's diagnosis was swift, as he informed his visitors that their son had been 'witched to the grave.' The cure he offered was drastic. The parents were urged to dig a hole in the garden and to place their son in it. They were then instructed to put a sheet over him, to throw a few shovelfuls of earth into the hole, and then leave him for ten minutes, after which they were to take him out and place him back in his bed. The curse of the grave would then have no hold over him and he would be cured. We do not know whether the young man recovered after this ordeal.

Dafydd Jones, Brynhyfryd, a descendant of the Pantcoy family told me this story. In January 1836 a man from Saron came to Pantcoy pleading with Harris to attend to his sick daughter. He agreed, saddled his horse and made for Saron in the company of the father. A mile or so outside Cwrtycadno, Harries pulled his horse to a sudden stop and, turning to the father, said that there was no point in going any further, as his daughter had died within the last few minutes. The disbelieving father galloped post-haste home to discover that his daughter had indeed died at the time stated by the Doctor. It is virtually impossible to prove the truth of such tales which have long been preserved in folk memory, but they all served to maintain the legend of the 'wizard of Pantcoy.'

One tale, for example, concerns a young woman who rushed from the chapel one Sunday in a state of madness. No one could cure her, so the father rode the forty miles or so to Pantcoy to ask for help. The Doctor informed the father that his daughter had been bewitched by an old woman. He showed him the whole scene in a magic mirror and then presented him with piece of paper upon which he had written some words. This paper was to be placed on his daughter's breast, so that the evil spirit would be forced to depart and she would be cured. Once again, it is not known whether the girl benefited from this bizarre cure.

Another story concerns a farmer from Cil-y-cwm who believed that his cows had been 'witched.' They would not touch the grass in their own field, but would eagerly feed elsewhere. Harries told him to buy a new knife, and then cut a piece of mountain ash with it. After that, he should burn some of the ash along with some cow's hair and butter in the fire. The guilty person would then appear at the door or window of the house, thereafter the cattle would graze contentedly on their own field.

Yet another account was recalled by a William Pritchard of Gwenddwr, who actually visited Pantcoy. An old man was struck down with the creeping palsy and Pritchard went with the man's grandson to see Harries. When they got there, he was standing at the gate but before they could say anything he said, 'You've been a long time coming; you can go back, the old man's time is over. If you had come sooner, I might have saved him. Tell him to make his peace, he has something heavy on his mind.' As both he and the grandson looked somewhat sceptical, Harries told them, 'I believe you think that I have friends who warned me of your coming. Maybe I have, but maybe I see for myself at a great distance.' Then he told Pritchard, 'I see a great white scar below your knee.' They both returned home and, unsurprisingly, the old man had died as predicted by the Doctor, but there was no indication of the scar. At harvest time Pritchard was on a rick, and as the last load arrived he slipped and landed upon a scythe cutting his knee to the bone. The resultant scar was exactly where Harries had said it would be. Pritchard added that he had 'great respect for Harries ever since.'

As we have seen, Harries was not averse to demonstrating his supernatural powers in a graphic manner. This was particularly the case when his abilities were questioned. After a certain vicar had the temerity to dismiss him as a fraud, the Doctor immediately took up the challenge. He prepared three sealed envelopes and sent them to the vicar, claiming that they contained the names of the next three persons to die within his parish. When within a week an old lady who had been ailing for a long time died, curiosity overtook the vicar and he opened the envelope. Naturally enough, the old lady's name had been enclosed. This did not impress the vicar overmuch as anyone could have predicted her death. When a few weeks later a young girl in the prime of life died unexpectedly, the clergyman was unnerved to find her name in the second envelope. Curiosity then led him to open the third envelope, and he was mortified to find that the name on the paper was his own. He tried to shrug the whole thing off as an attempt on the part of the Doctor to frighten him, but in the space of three months, his health had deteriorated, and soon he was seriously ill. The parishioners were aware of the challenge laid down by Harries, and when the vicar was the third one to die in the parish, many became convinced that he was the possesssor of supernatural powers.

Not all were taken in by the claims of Dr John Harries and his son Henry, who also claimed to have inherited his father's gifts. Ironically, although the family were practitioners of the esoteric arts, they were also practising Methodists. My attention was drawn by Mr John Jones, Pentre Cŵn, to the fact that the Pantcoy family contributed generously to the chapel at Caeo. The sons of the Doctor and his wife Letitia were even baptised in the chapel. One of his books in the National Library of Wales has this inscription in his own hand:

John Harries, Surgeon, his hand and pen. God give him health tonight again.

In spite of his Faustian reputation, he must have paid regard to more conventional beliefs.

The Methodists were particularly wary of those who practised the black arts. They inveighed against sorcerers, wizards, magicians and astrologers and were concerned that the sale of almanacs outstripped the sale of Bibles among their adherents. In 1801, a warning went out to the most credulous of their members not to be taken in by such

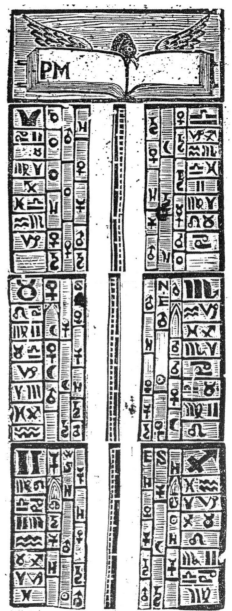

A sample of the many strange manuscripts of Dr John and his son, Henry Harries.

superstitions. This is illustrated by the experience of a father from Llanddewibrefi. His son was seriously ill, the flow of blood from his nose could not be stemmed, so he asked the members of his chapel to pray for his recovery. As there was no improvement, and now desperate for a cure, he crossed the mountain to Pantcoy. On this occasion, the Doctor told him that he was unable to help. Returning to Llanddewibrefi, the despondent father turned again to his fellow chapel members and asked them to pray for a miracle. This time, however, he was rebuffed by the deacons because he had turned his back on conventional religion and had sought to commune with a disciple of the devil in the person of Dr John Harries.

There is no doubt that he was shrewd and intuitive with a strong hold on the minds of those who turned to him at times of sickness and other tribulations. But some were more sceptical of his powers and accused him of duping people. It was claimed by some that his ploy was to hide when he saw visitors coming along the path to Pantcoy. The maid would show them to the parlour and would question them closely about their reasons for wishing to see the Doctor. He would listen to this conversation in an adjacent room, and when armed with the facts of the case, he would emerge professing to have prior knowledge of all their circumstances. This would impress those who sought his assistance and would be regarded as proof of his extraordinary powers. On the other hand, it might be that he had a capacity to 'read people' and had learned the art of mental manipulation. In an age when superstition was rife it would not be too difficult to convince people that he had magical powers.

The most fierce opponent of John Harries and his son was David Owen whose pen name was 'Brutus'. An ardent Anglican, he was the editor of *Yr Haul*. Incensed at the claims made by Henry Harries in the following card, he attacked him in the columns of *Yr Haul* and ridiculed wizards and astrologers in general.

Nativities Calculated.
In which are given the general Transactions of the Native through life, viz. Description (without seeing the person) Temper, Disposition, Fortunate or Unfortunate in their general pursuits; Honour, Riches, Journeys and Voyages (success therein and what places best to travel to, or reside in); Friends and Enemies, Trade or Profession best to

follow; and whether fortunate in Speculations, viz. Lottery, Dealing in Foreign markets etc.

Of marriage, if to marry – The Description, Temper and Disposition of the Person, from whence rich or poor, happy or unhappy in marriage etc. etc. Of Children, whether fortunate or not etc. etc. Deduced from the influence of the Sun and Moon with the Planetary Orbs at the time of Birth. Also in Sickness and Diseases etc.

By Henry Harries

All letters addressed to him or his father Mr. John Harries, Cwrtycadno, must be post paid, or not received.

Owen found all these claims risible, but he was concerned that the more gullible in society might well be taken in by them. He launched a series of diatribes aimed at Henry Harries, but his venom was also directed towards his father. Some have held that his bitter attacks resulted from his own frustration at failing to become a doctor, but it is hard to accept this. Brutus had already earned a reputation as a trenchant critic of all that he deemed to be hypocritical as is evidenced by the following words:

Yr ydym wedi clywed am nifer lluosog o dwyllwyr ym mhob oes, y rhai yn effeithiol a llwyddiannus a gawsant gan y werinos gredu eu hudoliaeth, ond y mae rhyw haerllugrwydd a chythreuldeb yng ngharden Henry Harries ymhell o'r tu hwnt i ddim a gynnigiwyd erioed.

('We have heard of a large number of deceivers in every age, some who were effective and successful have managed to persuade the ordinary people of their magic, but there is some impudence and devilry in Henry Harries's card which goes beyond anything that has been offered before.')

Mae Mr. Henry Harries wedi cyfansoddi ei hun fel Tywysog Fortunetellers y ddaear . . . yn proffesu yn y garden y gall roddi gwybodaeth ynghylch pethau dyfodadwy oddiwrth effaith yr haul, y lleuad, a'r planedau ar amser genedigaeth . . . A fu ef yn ymddiddan a'r haul? . . . Neu ynte ai dyn y lleuad a ddysgodd hon iddo? . . . Ef yn gwybod am dynghedfen dyn! Gwyr yr un faint am hynny a mwngci o Gibraltar neu barot o Ceylon.

('Mr Henry Harries has presented himself as the Prince of the earth's Fortunetellers . . . claiming that he can provide information about future things from the effect of the sun, the moon and the planets at the time of birth . . . Did he converse with the sun? . . . Or perhaps it was the man in the moon who taught him this? . . . He knows as much about it as a monkey from Gibraltar or a parrot from Ceylon.')

Mae'n drueni mawr bod cynnifer o ffyliaid yn ein plith yn credu hudoliaeth Henry Harries a'i gyffelyb, y rhai nad oes ganddynt ddim mewn golwg ond twyllo dynion a gwneuthur ffyliaid yn ffolach.

('It is a great pity that so many fools among us believe in the magic of Henry Harries and his like, who have nothing in mind but to deceive men and to make fools even more foolish.')

Someone under the pseudonym 'Cymro Cloff' wrote this verse attacking Henry Harries in *Yr Haul* entitled *Myfyrdod wrth ddychwelyd o Gwrt y Cadno* ('Meditation on returning from Cwrt y Cadno'):

Ffarwel fo i Henry Harries
A'i hespion lyfrau hyspys
A'i ffug, a'i odiaeth weniaith wan
I dwyllo'r anneallus.

('Farewell to Henry Harries with his dry magical books, and his false and weak flattery in order to deceive the ignorant'.)

In spite of David Owen's attempts at exposing John and Henry Harries as charlatans, those he regarded as fools still trekked to Pantcoy to seek their services. In his essay on *Ghost Raising in Wales,* Jonathan Ceredig Davies, the folklorist, quoting Glendower in Shakespeare's *Henry IV, Part One* ('I can raise spirits from the vasty deep'), maintained that the ability to cause spirits to appear was believed in parts of Wales even at the turn of the last century. He searched the Library at Pantcoy in 1905, and discovered many 'curious' things, including this invocation which was deemed to have been used by Harries in calling upon the spirit world.

How to obtain the Familiar of the Genius or Good Spirit and cause him to appear – let him compose an earnest prayer unto the said

Genius, which he must repeat thrice every morning for seven days before the Invocation . . . on the day of the Invocation he must enter a private closet having a little table, and silk carpet, and two waxen candles lighted – and a crystal dome shaped triangularly the size of an apple – fixed in the centre of the table . . . he must consecrate the candles, the carpet, the table and the crystal with a sprinkling of his own blood.

The supplicant is then required to recite the names of innumerable ancient deities and wait patiently for the appearance of the Genius . . .

. . . about a quarter of an hour before, a great variety of apparitions appear as a beaten road or track and travellers men and women marching silently along, next, rivers, wells, mountains and seas . . . a shepherd upon a pleasant hill feeding his sheep with the sun shining brightly – birds and beasts and monsters which vanish with the coming of the Genius.

Harries did not restrict his dalliances with the spirits to the privacy of his own closet. He set out to encourage the belief that he was no ordinary healer but one who was not 'in the roll of common men.' He indulged in the theatrical and took part in bizarre rituals designed to convince the more gullible that he was indeed the possessor of extraordinary gifts. According to tradition, he would choose a clearing in the woods, and wearing a white gown, he would draw three circles. Standing inside these circles, he would sprinkle holy water and, holding a candle, he would begin an incantation calling upon Jehovah, the saints and the heavenly bodies to assist him. It was also claimed that these rituals would be accompanied by thunder and lightning, thus adding an authenticity to the Doctor's claims. In an age of superstition, when belief in such phenomena as corpse candles was common, it took little to convince people that the 'wizard of Pantcoy' was indeed able to converse with the spirits and demons. Many of those who went to Pantcoy spoke of seeing figures materialising before their very eyes. One man who asked for advice concerning his future bride, claimed that he had seen her face reflected in a mirror. Was he hallucinating, had he been hypnotised, or did the Doctor truly possess paranormal powers?

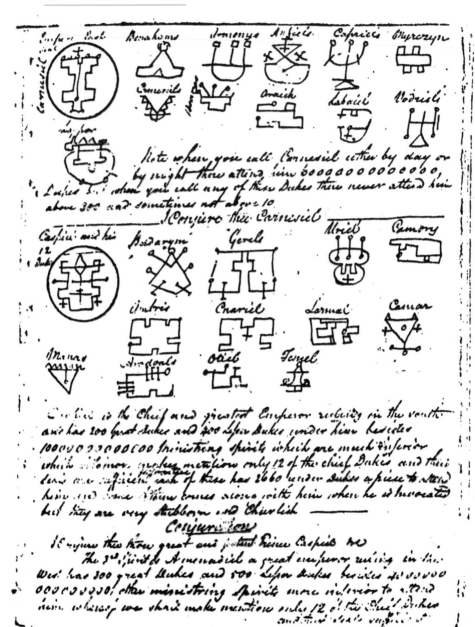

Dr Harries's Holograph Book.

It was also believed locally that Dr. Harries derived his powers from a large stone, which can still be seen today. On this stone he would stand and call upon those spirits who would enable him to foretell events. It was shown to me some years ago by Mr Dafydd Jones, Brynhyfryd, who told me that it was still referred to as 'Carreg Dr John Harries' ('Dr John Harries's Stone') He pointed to certain holes drilled in the stone by local people. They had apparently filled them with gunpowder in an attempt to break up the stone to see whether it would reveal any of its secrets. Fortunately, or unfortunately, they did not succeed, so the secrets of Dr Harries were safe and never brought into the open. Many of his actions, however, may have resulted from guile rather than magic. When called to Glansevin mansion near Llangadog to identify a thief who had stolen a gold ring, all the servants were lined up and Harries gave each one a twig of equal length. He told them to take them to their bedrooms, and the following morning he would inspect them again. If the thief was among them, his or her twig would have grown the length of a thumbnail. When he inspected the twigs he found that one had been shortened by this length, and thus he was able to identify the thief.

Other examples of his capacity to identify thieves are mentioned by Marie Trevelyan. One such tale refers to a man from Pontarddulais who lost £10 and in despair he went to Pantcoy. He was told by the Doctor that the money was hidden under a pile of rags in a cupboard and that it had been stolen by a relative. The man returned home and was able to find the money and identify the thief. Another story which she claimed to be 'well authenticated' concerns two men who went to Swansea to sell their corn. Money from the sale was kept by one of them in his pocket, but on their way home they fell asleep in the cart and on waking found that the money was gone. After a fruitless search, they visited the Doctor who led them into a room and placed a round mirror in front of them. Instead of seeing their own reflections, they saw their own images sleeping in the cart. They then saw a neighbour, who had hitherto been above suspicion, taking the money. Sometimes the Doctor would inflict his own punishment on a thief, as happened in the case of a farmer from Glamorgan who lost £100 following the sale of his cattle. Harries told him that the money had been stolen and was hidden in a bag. He went further and told him that he would punish the thief and cause him to be confined to his bed for twelve months. The farmer recovered the bag, but a few days later a neighbouring farmer was taken ill and sometime later confessed that he had no rest because the Doctor kept coming to him in his sleep, urging him to confess and to restore the money to its rightful owner.

We have already seen that his son Henry Harries claimed to base many of his predictions on astrology, a study which retains a certain respectability in some quarters even today. Many notable personages in history have placed their faith in astrological predictions, including Elizabeth I and Adolf Hitler. It was even claimed that Ronald Reagan's wife, Nancy, advised him on the basis of such predictions. The library at Pantcoy had many books on occultism and horoscopes. The collection of the Pantcoy papers at the National Library of Wales also contain many charts relating to the sun, the moon and the stars. But one book is missing. It appears that Dr Harries and his son had a *Llyfr Mawr*, a Large Book in which he kept details of all his occult practices and rituals. This was always kept under lock and key. The late Mrs Willams of Cwrtycadno worked at Pantcoy at the turn of the last century, and recalled seeing such a book in the house. One day, however, a stranger came to the farm and asked to see the library, and after his departure it was noticed that the book had disappeared and it has not been seen since. An account in the Transactions of the Carmarthenshire Antiquarian Society also testifies to the existence of such a book. There, it is claimed that no member of the family would dare touch it, but that it was eventually bought by a London barrister who visited Pantcoy. So, whatever the fate of the book, we are left to ponder what secrets were contained within its covers.

In spite of the scepticism of David Owen, a large number still turned to Pantcoy to seek assistance. Some travelled long distances to Cwrtycadno, others sent their requests by letter. This letter sent to Henry Harries is typical:

> Dear Sir,
> My sister desire that you to do the best for her. Mary Ann have a pain in the bust – will you please send a resit (sic) for it. Mary Ann was born May 20 or 24 – it was on Sunday at 4 o clock in the morning in the year 1823. – lives at Cilbedog, Crickcadarn, Brecs.

Catherine Lloyd was born August 23 at 20 mins past 11 in the fournoon (sic) 1830 – lives at Pentwyn, Cwmdu, Brecs.

Please to send it down in a leter and the price – we will send the money by Post Office order or I will bring it up.

Yours truly,

William Lloyd

We do not know whether Henry Harries was able to help.

Another letter from a somewhat confused suitor asked for advice about marriage:

Sir,

I have sent these few lines to you, as an old friend of mine I have rote (sic) to, a curten purson (sic) and have spoke to her once. I do not know is that purson (sic) to be my weded wife or not. I shall leve (sic) it to you to judge. She lives south west of here where I do live – about 11 miles distance nr. Abergavenny. If it is any other in another quarter, please to leave me know in a note from you by the bearer Daniel Jones.

Yours,

Thomas Thomas

It was not only the superstitious 'common folk' who turned to the Harrieses. There are letters from a Captain Thomas of Newport, Pembs, seeking a cure for his wife, and a Captain Griffith from Cardigan pleading on behalf of a sick sister.

Those who visited Pantcoy for assistance were given amulets or paper charms to ward off misfortune. These were to protect them from spells and curses. Many came to request the intervention of Dr Harries and his son at times of misfortune when animals fell sick, or when the milk turned sour, or the butter refused to churn. They were also given this slip of paper with the words

O Lord Jesus, I beseech thee, preserve the cows, calves, horses . . . the milk, the cream, the cheese, the butter from the power of all evil, man, woman, or devilish spirits.

Armed with this they felt safe, protected from harm and from the curses or spells of malicious neighbours.

The belief in his capacity to predict future events placed him above the realms of common men in the minds of local people. In Cwrtycadno, it was believed that he had foretold the tragic events that would occur in the mansion at Dolaucothi. In 1876, such an event occurred. The much respected Judge Johnes was shot by his butler Henry Tremble. Today, the Judge and, probably, the murderer Tremble, lie in the churchyard at Caeo where Harries was buried.

Dr Harries's Death Certificate.

However adept Dr. John Harries was at curing others, he could not forestall his own demise. He died on 14 May, 1839, aged fifty-four. As moss gathers around a stone, so stories have gathered around the circumstances of his death. One such story maintains that he had predicted the time and date of his passing, but that when the day duly arrived, he was determined to defy his own prediction. He decided to spend the day in bed so that no accident or misfortune could befall him. As he lay there cocooned from all harm, the thatched roof of Pantcoy caught fire and he was forced to rush out. He climbed a ladder to extinguish the fire, but in doing so, he fell and was killed, thus fulfilling his own prediction. This would have made a marvellous end to the story of the 'Wizard of Pantcoy'. Unfortunately, the facts may not bear this out. On checking his death certificate in Carmarthen, I found that the cause of death is given as 'the decay', in other words, tuberculosis. He had attended to so many others who had fallen victim to this disease, but in this case the physician had failed to heal himself. This was a common disease in the family and his son Henry also succumbed to it. He was visited by Thomas Jenkins of Llandeilo who noted in his diary: 'Went to see Henry Harris the astrologer . . . He is in a decline, cant live many weeks'.

pic. Tim Jones   The church and churchyard at Caeo.

John Harries's funeral could be no ordinary funeral, it had to be adorned with a degree of melodrama. It is claimed that as the cortège wound its way to Caeo churchyard, a herd of cows in a nearby field became afflicted with a kind of madness. They escaped and careered for about four miles without stopping until they reached Pwll Uffern ('Hell's Pool'). As the cortège reached Rhiw Llwyn Ceiliog, the bearers claimed that the heavy coffin suddenly became much lighter. The belief was, that as the devil had already taken his soul as payment for his special gifts, he had now returned to claim his body as well. Jonathan Ceredig Davies refers to this story, but he also noted that a similar claim was made when a '*dyn hysbys*' was buried in Llanafan churchyard in 1863. He added that his 'informant' was present on that occasion. All this points to the fact that the lives of 'cunning men' such as Dr. Harries were subsequently embroidered, in an attempt to preserve their mystique and to explain the undoubted gifts that they possessed. Inevitably, these were exaggerated and gilded by the telling, but they still provide for us an interesting collection of folk tales. Whatever the truth or otherwise of such tales, the Wizard of Pantcoy had received a Christian baptism from Eliezer Williams M.A., the son of the renowned biblical scholar Peter Williams, who served as Vicar of Caeo. Later he became head of the renowned grammar school at Lampeter. Harries was also accorded a Christian burial with the Reverend D. Price Lewis, Curate of Llanycrwys officiating.

After John Harries's death, his son Henry carried on the family business. An astute businessman, his emphasis was more upon astrological predictions. His father had undertaken the role of surgeon, physician, apothecary and seer all rolled into one. Although admired for his medical expertise, he received a cautious respect tinged with a modicum of fear for his other skills. Unfortunately, Henry Harries did not enjoy robust health throughout his life, and he died at the age of forty-two on 19 June, 1849. Today, the Harrieses lie in the tranquillity of Caeo churchyard, if indeed the body of the Doctor was interred! He was buried with his father, who was known as Henry Shon Harri, but on the gravestone an anglicised version of the name is inscribed. The Doctor had chosen Harries rather than Jones as his surname and his profession is described as a surgeon.

In Memory
Of
Henry Jones, Pantcoy, who died
August 6, 1805 Aged 66 years
Also
of his son John Harries
Pantcoy, Surgeon, who died
May 11 1839
Aged 54 years

Dr John Harries's gravestone.   *pic. Tim Jones*

In the lives of Dr John Harries and his son Henry, the boundaries between fact and fiction are often blurred. In our sophisticated age with its advances in medical science, the actions of seers and healers are viewed with a great deal of suspicion. Even so, the names of Dr John Harries and his son Henry live to this day, and they are still regarded as two of the last great Welsh wizards. Whether they were genuine healers or unscrupulous charlatans must, however, remain an open question. Even so, their fame or notoriety was such, that they were deemed important enough to have their names included in the Dictionary of National Biography, an honour accorded to few 'wizards and astrologers.'

CHAPTER FIVE

THE SIN OF MARY PROUT

Murder can never be glorified, nor indeed justified, but sometimes it can be understood. The tragedy, therefore, of young Mary Prout evokes sympathy rather than anger, although she committed the ultimate crime. It was not greed, revenge or even hatred that brought her to this, but a sense of utter helplessness and despair in an age when prejudice and neglect were rife.

Mary was born in December, 1842, the third child of Thomas and Mary Prout of Amroth, Pembrokeshire. Her father was a collier in the local coal mine, but sadly, her mother died at the young age of thirty-nine giving birth to a fourth child, Rhoda. Now deprived of a mother, the children were brought up by their grandmother and their father, who belonged to the sect known as the Primitive Methodists. Thus, they had a strict religious upbringing, but Mary and her sister Rhoda were baptised in the Parish Church of St. Elidyr.

As Mary had very little formal education, her prospects extended no further than to serve as a lowly maid in a large house in Saundersfoot. In 1863, however, she became pregnant and was immediately asked to leave, such was the stigma attached to a young girl who found herself in such a predicament. She refused to divulge the name of the father, and having nowhere else to turn, she returned to the home of her grand-parents. Her own father was outraged by the situation and rejected his daughter completely, but her grandmother allowed her to stay at her cottage for a few months. This was a short respite, for soon we find a heavily pregnant Mary trudging disconsolately from Amroth towards Narberth, a distance of eight miles. With her few possessions, she neared the forbidding and unwelcoming doors of the Union Workhouse, dubbed the Bastille, the last refuge for those in her situation. It was viewed locally with a mixture of fear and hatred and so great were these emotions towards it that it had been attacked by the Rebecca Rioters some twenty years previously and set on fire. Later, it was set on fire for a second time.

The Workhouse at Narberth served a radius of about ten miles; its grim building reminded one more of a prison than a supposedly caring institution. But a purpose lay behind this, because there was a supposition that the travails of those who sought its sanctuary were, on the whole, self-inflicted and poverty itself was held to be a sin. The Workhouse, known locally as the Union, was run by the Master, John Williams, with his wife Martha as the Matron. They earned £70 per annum and were, on the whole, well off. For the inmates, however, it was another story. Discipline was rigid, and the many petty rules and regulations stripped them of their individuality, their self-esteem, and self-respect. They were never allowed to forget that they were totally reliant upon the charity of others.

As Mary tentatively sought entry on 12 February, 1844, and as the heavy doors clanged shut behind her, she was to enter a world where she would be reminded on a daily basis that she was a sinner stripped of all her dignity. The control of the Workhouse was in the hands of the Board of Guardians who were ever conscious of the need to curtail costs, thus relieving the burden on the parishioners. After all, charity had its limits. The feelings of the unfortunate inmates rarely featured as a priority. The sexes were separated, and husbands and wives were forced, even in old age, to end their days living apart. There was a general fear of disease, particularly of cholera, which was rife. On entry, Mary would have been 'thoroughly cleansed with carbolic soap' and, to complete the dehumanising process, she was issued with her distinctive workhouse uniform. This consisted of a striped linen frock, a smock, a pinafore and a calico cap. Since Mary was unable to read or write, the Matron read out the innumerable regulations that she had to observe. Such a catalogue of rules must have left Mary even more traumatised. Here are a few examples:

Moved by Mr Biddulph Seconded by Mr Leach that the following
Dietary be adopted for able bodied Paupers of this Union

		Breakfast				Dinner						Suppers			
		Bread	Cheese	Gruel or Pottage	Milk	Bread	Cheese	Cooked Meat Potatoes vegetables	Soup	British Rice	Milk	Bread	Cheese	Potatoes	Milk
		oz	oz	Pints	Pints	oz	oz	oz	oz	Pints	oz	Pints	oz	oz	oz	Pints
Sunday	Men	7	"	"	1	"	"	5	16	"	"	"	7	2	"	.
	Women	7	"	"	1	"	"	5	16	"	"	"	7	2	"	"
Monday	Men	7	"	1½	"	7	"	"	"	1½	"	"	"	"	16	1
	Women	7	"	1½	"	7	"	"	.	1½	"	"	"	"	16	1
Tuesday	Men	7	"	"	1	"	"	16	1½	"	"	7	2	"	"
	Women	7	"	"	1	"	"	"	16	1½	"	"	7	2	"	"
Wednesday	Men	7	2	"	"	"	"	"	"	"	12	1	7	2	"	"
	Women	7	2	"	"	"	"	"	"	"	12	1	7	2	"	"
Thursday	Men	7	"	"	1	7	"	"	"	1½	"	"	"	2	16	"
	Women	7	"	"	1	7	"	"	"	1½	"	"	"	2	16	"
Friday	Men	7	"	1½	"	"	"	"	16	1½	"	"	7	"	"	1
	Women	7	"	1½	"	"	"	"	16	1½	"	"	7	"	"	1
Saturday	Men	7	"	1½	"	7	"	"	"	1½	"	"	"	2	16	"
	Women	7	"	1½	"	7	"	"	"	1½	"	"	"	2	16	"

Old People, of Sixty years of age and upwards may be allowed 1 oz of Tea
5 oz of Butter and 7 oz of Sugar per week in lieu of Gruel
Soup Pottage or Milk for Breakfast ——

The Workhouse rations.

Article 1 Any pauper who shall neglect to observe such of the rules and regulations of the Poor Law Commission as are applicable or binding on him or her.

Or shall make a noise when silence is ordered.

Or shall use obscene or profane language.

Or shall by word or deed insult . . . any other person.

Or shall threaten to strike or assault a person.

Or shall not duly cleanse his or her person.

Or shall refuse or neglect work.

Or shall pretend sickness.

Or shall enter . . . without permission the ward or yard appropriated to a class of paupers, other than to which he or she belongs.

Or shall wilfully disobey any lawful order of any officer of the workhouse.

Or shall be drunk.

Or shall commit an act of indecency.

Or shall by act or deed insult the master or matron, or any other officer of the workhouse or any Guardian of the Union . . .

Her pregnant state did not absolve Mary from hard work. Within a day of her admission, she was toiling at the repetitive tasks of cleaning the floors, sewing, knitting, laundrywork and, the worst of all, picking oakum. This involved separating the strands of old ropes which could cut her fingers causing them to bleed. Any inmate refusing to work was locked in a cell and fed bread and water. Mary Prout was not one to defy authority, for in the records she is described by the Matron as a 'civil and orderly inmate who caused no trouble'.

Fortunately, there existed among some of the inmates a camaraderie which provided a degree of protection for young and vulnerable inmates like Mary. She was befriended by Hester Thomas, a hardened long-time resident. Already the mother of three children, she was again pregnant and like Mary had been placed in the so-called 'lying-in ward'. Knowing all the ropes, she pitied the anxious Mary and took her under her wing. But, even she could not protect her from the rigours of workhouse life with its frugal diet of porridge, *cawl*, limited portions of bread, cheese, potatoes and a little meat twice a week. The *Times* reporter T.C. Foster examined a typical workhouse diet at Carmarthen and described it thus,

The bread which I saw and tested is made entirely of barley and nearly black. Three and a half ounces of meat on Sundays and Wednesdays and soup and milk gruel the rest of the week. Potatoes at one and a half pounds a day; an ounce and a half of cheese for supper and salt herring on Friday.

He concluded that the prisoners in Carmarthen Gaol were served better food than that provided for the inmates at Carmarthen Workhouse.

This was hardly a suitable diet for an expectant mother already weakened by her ordeal. On 9 April, Mary went into labour and the following day she gave birth to a baby girl, who was called Rhoda after her deceased sister. Following her confinement, the Matron noted that Mary seemed very depressed as she felt that her baby was not thriving. She later testified that,

Mary was very civil, but very reserved: when I went into the room she would speak if spoken to, but not without. She paid every attention she could to the child, but it did not thrive very well. She seemed fond of it. But I did notice that Mary was distressed at the child not thriving.

Hesther Thomas also gave evidence regarding Mary's mental state.

I did notice that she was distressed that the child had the red gum . . . I saw the child every day – she paid every attention she could as far as I know. She seemed fond of the baby.

Every child born at the Workhouse had to be registered. James Davies, the Registrar of Slebech, was called three weeks after Rhoda's birth and he later testified.

I attended at the Narberth Union on 2 May, 1864. I registered a child there . . . she (Mary Prout) made a statement to me, She gave me the information I put down here in the Register. The date of the birth was 19th April, 1864. The place of birth was the Workhouse, Narberth. The name of the child Rhoda. No father. Mary Prout mother. The mark X of Mary Prout as informant. I read this to her and then she made her mark.

On 13 May, Mary was allowed out of the Workhouse to visit her grandmother, from whom she collected some clothes for the baby. She was allowed out at 7am but had to return by 7pm. With her three-week-old child wrapped in a shawl, Mary would have to walk a total distance of sixteen miles that day. She returned with a little cotton shift, a cotton handkerchief, a binder, a flannel petticoat and a frock. But she also returned totally exhausted and debilitated and was distressed to learn that her time at the Workhouse would be limited.

Because she had a grandmother, the Guardians felt that they could not extend their 'charity' towards Mary and the baby for very much longer. They, after all, were the custodians of the meagre sums of money devoted to looking after the paupers, and if they could pass the responsibility to others, all well and good. The limited means and the age of the grandmother, and her scant ability to look after Mary and her child, was not their concern. Consequently, Mary was told that she had to leave the Workhouse at the end of the week. For Mary this was devastating news. In spite of its harsh limitations, it had provided Mary and her sickly child with a much needed sanctuary, and she had also been buoyed by the advice and friendship of Hester Thomas. Abandoned by her father, she would now be totally dependent upon the charity of her aged grandmother. Although she had been prepared to help at the outset, her strong religious convictions still made it difficult for her to forgive a granddaughter who had brought so much shame on the family. Martha Williams, the Matron, appreciated Mary's predicament and tried to persuade the Guardians to let her stay, but to no avail. Considerations of cost would supersede her entreaties: from now on Mary would not be their concern.

On 20 May, Mary Prout and the six-week-old Rhoda were forced to leave the Workhouse late in the afternoon to face an alien and uncaring world. Burdened with a crying infant in a shawl, and carrying a meagre bundle of possessions, she started out on the long journey to Amroth. A tearful Hester Thomas bade her farewell and gave her a little cap that she had knitted for the baby as a leaving present. Ahead of her lay the unbridled prejudice of a society that looked down on those whose sin was giving birth to children out of wedlock. On the road to her grandmother's house, Mary met two people who were later to testify to the encounter. One was Hannah Davies of Colby Lodge who stated,

I know Mary Prout. On Friday, 20 May, I saw Mary Prout about twelve minutes past eight and met her close to my house in the field . . . She had a child in her arms . . . I passed the time of day with her – she had an air of sadness about her.

Her daughter also gave evidence,

I knew she was a Prout! I stopped to talk to her. I said she had a pretty baby. She said, 'It keeps small'; The baby was sucking at the time.

Mary's last bond with the child was to sit in a field in an attempt to feed it. When she eventually reached her grandmother's house at about 8.30pm, she was without the baby. Later, her grandmother was called to give evidence at an Inquest held at Saundersfoot.

I am a widow, I know Mary Prout I am her grandmother. Last Friday night about half past eight she came to my house she had no baby with her, she sat down and said well grandmother . . . I asked her where was her child, she burst out crying and said it was in the Narberth Union dead. I said do not cry, go on your knees Mary and give thanks to God for taking it. I asked her when she died. She said on Tuesday evening. I asked her if it was buried, she said no, not until Saturday. I never saw it from the time it died; she ate no supper; she slept with me all night. That is all she said about the child. She left on Saturday morning, she said she was going to see her sister. I live at Summerhill, the Little Pit is about a mile from there. She had breakfast and hurried away in the morning.

Mary's return without the baby inevitably gave rise to a great deal of gossip in the neighbourhood, and when it became apparent that it had not died in the Workhouse, suspicions were aroused. The area was pitted with mineshafts and a search was arranged. To those who had spoken to Mary she had seemed traumatised, and she was still unable or unwilling to throw any light upon the whereabouts of Rhoda. The Police Sergeant at Saundersfoot had been informed by a local miner that the baby might be found near Colby Lodge, but after searching the fields and hedgerows he found nothing. He then sought the assistance of two local miners who went down a pit known as the Little Pit; finally, on 22 May, the mystery of Rhoda's disappearance was solved and the real extent of the tragedy revealed. William Davies, the husband of Hannah Davies who had spoken to Mary earlier, descended into the pit accompanied by his son. They were both miners, and he later described what they found.

> I found the body of a child – it was lying on its right side at the bottom of the pit: I brought the baby up, it had a cap on, but the skull was smashed. The baby was placed in a bucket and hauled up.

In the meantime, Mary had made her way to her sister's house at Law Street in Pembroke Dock. Following the discovery of Rhoda's body, the wheels of justice now swung into full motion. At four in the morning on 23 May there was loud knocking on the door of the house in Law Street, and Superintendent Kelly on entering the house found Mary in bed with her sister. He immediately arrested her and in his later evidence he described the subsequent events.

> I charged her with the murder of her child by throwing it into a pit on the Friday previous. She wanted to talk and I cautioned her not to talk. I conveyed her to Pembroke Lock Up. She remained there until one o' clock. Then I took her to Saundersfoot. She said, 'If they hang me I will tell them the truth: I threw it and ran away a short distance, then I returned and found there was no noise.' I took down what she said – she had nothing to eat from 4 a.m. until evening, she was offered food but she would not take it.

Mary was in a piteous condition and continued to blurt out that she had been driven to kill the child out of anxiety and despair. Thomas Newsam, the surgeon at Saundersfoot, confirmed that the baby had died from a fractured skull. He also testified that he had previously known Mary when she was a domestic servant in the house at Saundersfoot where he had lodged for nine months. He described her as a 'quiet, easy, good natured girl', and confirmed that he had observed nothing in her character which would have predisposed her to insanity. An inquest into Rhoda's death was held at Saundersfoot and after listening to the evidence the jury returned a verdict of 'wilful murder' against Mary Prout, when she was committed under the Coroner's Warrant to Haverfordwest gaol to be tried at the next Assizes.

Mary was taken under escort to await her trial for the capital offence of murder. A month or so later, the Assizes were held with due ceremony at Haverfordwest at which,

> Mary Prout, Spinster, aged 22 was indicted for the wilful murder of Rhoda Prout in the parish of Amroth on 20, May 1864. Mr. Henry Allen and Mr. De Rutzen conducted the prosecution and Mr. Thomas Allen defended the prisoner.

She stood in the dock, a frail and vulnerable young girl surrounded by the bewigged lawyers, appearing before a jury of her peers and facing the stern and robed figure of the judge. From the public gallery, the curious townspeople craned their necks to catch a glimpse of the prisoner who had committed the most heinous of crimes. The case for the prosecution did not take very long. Mary had already confessed that she had killed her baby, but Mr Thomas Allen for the defence made an excellent but vain attempt to plead on her behalf. He contended that as there were no witnesses to the act there was no absolute proof that she had an intention to kill her own baby. He stressed that the baby had been in very poor health when Mary left the Workhouse. It had been weak and ailing since birth, and there was no certainty that it would have survived for much longer. Consequently, he held that it was impossible to prove beyond reasonable doubt that the baby had not suffered convulsions and that it was already dead before Mary had thrown it into the pit. He argued that if there was a scintilla of doubt in the minds of the jury, it should work for the benefit of the prisoner. He also argued that even if they believed that the baby was alive, they should take into account the state of mind of the prisoner who had been exposed to so much neglect and ill treatment before and after the birth of her child.

In his summing up the judge directed the jury on the law relating to cases of infanticide, which equated to the crime of murder. They had to consider whether or not there was an intention to kill the child, and whether in doing so she was of sound mind at the time and therefore responsible for her action. Increasingly, juries were reluctant to convict young girls of infanticide, knowing what the ultimate penalty could be. In some cases, assumptions were made that the baby had been born dead thus allowing for the lesser charge of concealing the body to be brought. Mary could not take advantage of this, as the Workhouse records and subsequent sightings proved otherwise. Even after conviction for infanticide and the pronouncement of the death sentence, those found guilty were only hanged in rare circumstances. But it remained a possibility. In Wales, the most notorious example was the hanging in 1805 of Mary Morgan, aged seventeen, at Presteigne for killing her illegitimate baby. Post-natal depression and the 'shame' of giving birth to a child outside marriage were not deemed to be relevant defences. Infanticide was murder pure and simple. It was not until the Infanticide Acts of 1922 and 1938 that such matters could be taken into account as mitigating factors. In those cases where the death penalty was commuted, life imprisonment was the only alternative punishment.

After retiring and deliberating at some length, the jury returned to the court and delivered their verdict. While acknowledging the affection that Mary had for the baby and while accepting that the act had been an impulsive one without possible premeditation, they, nevertheless, found her guilty of murder. They did, however, add a plea for mercy in the hope that she would be spared the ultimate penalty. The judge, representing the full authority of the Law of England, had no course other than to don his black cap and intone the awful words that would possibly seal Mary Prout's fate.

> The sentence of the court is that you Mary Prout, be taken back to the Prison from whence you came, and thence on a date to be determined, to a place of execution, and that you be hanged by the neck until you are dead, and that your body be buried within the precincts of the Gaol.

The judge's chaplain then added the chilling words:

> And may the Lord God Almighty have mercy on your soul.

W.D. Phillips, a local author, who was present in the court, recalls the reaction of Mary Prout to her sentence.

I was in the Assize Court when the Judge assumed the black cap and a murmur of horror emanated from most of the women present. All eyes turned on the trembling girl in the dock as the sentence of death was pronounced. It was a pitiable sight to see her grasp the dock rail with both hands.

Mary was removed from the dock 'moaning and crying piteously' and returned to her cell in Haverfordwest Gaol to await her fate. The Gaol Files record her admission.

Name: Mary Prout
Age: 22
Trade: Spinster Servant
Date of Warrant: 24th May 1864
When received into custody: 25th May 1864
Offence: Wilful murder of Rhoda Prout at the parish church of St Issells
When tried: 13th July 1864
Verdict of the Jury: Guilty of Murder
Sentence of the Court: Death.

For the next three weeks Mary languished in her cold and damp prison cell. She was guarded night and day lest any harm should come to her before the sentence of the court could be carried out. Tormented now by guilt and fear, she was scarcely able to eat. She had freely admitted her guilt and appeared resigned to her fate. In the meantime, arrangements would need to be made for her execution. This was a time when hangings were carried out in public and witnessed by thousands of curious spectators. Not until 1868, following so many unruly and disreputable scenes at hangings, was it decreed that they should take place within the prison walls. Prior to this a gallows would usually be erected outside the prison and the unfortunate prisoner exposed to the ghastly rituals which inevitably accompanied the event. It was heralded by the tolling of the prison bell as the solemn procession made its way towards the gallows. In many towns and cities, where such spectacles were common, execution days were often regarded as public holidays, but in a quiet country town such as Haverfordwest this was a rare

List of Prisoners and Offences.

spectacle. In fact, some forty years had elapsed since the last hanging in the town. A century earlier, Howel Harris, the Methodist revivalist, had witnessed a double execution during a visit to Haverfordwest. An elderly mother and her daughter were hanged for the murder of the daughter's baby, although they had pleaded their innocence to the end. They were both Welsh speakers from Newcastle Emlyn, a factor which could have limited their ability to defend themselves in court. Harris refers to the behaviour of the large and unruly mob watching the hanging. Prompted by this, he leapt onto the scaffold and standing beside the hangman he pointed to the bodies of the unfortunate victims and prayed. In his prayer, he exhorted the crowd to remember that Jesus had also hung from a cross in order to save them. It appears that this message was not well received.

The prospect of witnessing a young girl suffering the extreme penalty aroused conflicting emotions within the town. Many, including some prominent people, were appalled at the proposed execution, and rested their hopes on the recommendation of the jury that the prisoner should be spared the death penalty. Even the judge, Justice Crompton, seemed to be sympathetic to that view. One of the stoutest opponents of the death penalty was the Editor of the Haverfordwest and Milford Haven Chronicle, but there was in reality, very little time to save the life of Mary Prout. Executions were usually carried out after three clear Sundays had elapsed following the imposition of the death sentence. Arrangements for the hanging would normally be made by the Under Sheriff on behalf of the High Sheriff. The public hangman at this time was William Calcraft. He was an exponent of the 'short drop' which had not always proved to be the most efficient method of execution and had led to some quite horrific blunders. As a busy man, a date would have to be arranged with him. The fact that Mary was a young woman would not trouble him too unduly, for he had once hanged a seventeen-year-old girl in Bristol convicted of killing her sadistic mistress. A scaffold would have to be erected outside the prison wall and arrangements made to control the crowd expected to flock into the town to witness the event.

There was of course the prospect of an appeal. Arrangements were swiftly made to collect names for a petition to be submitted to the Home

The bell that called Mary Prout and the other inmates to work.

By kind permission of the National Library of Wales.

Office requesting that the sentence of death imposed upon Mary be respited. In a strongly-worded article, the Editor of the Haverfordwest and Milford Haven Chronicle argued against the death penalty in general. This was a courageous stand in an age when such views were very much in the minority. He strongly contested its deterrent effect.

> The argument that men are deterred from the commission of a crime by the dread of death is singularly false – false because the fear of death is an unrealizable feeling in living men, and hence utterly inoperative . . . public executions are not deterrent examples and produce in the breasts of the majority of spectators no dislike to the criminal and no abhorrence of the crime, it is a sad and solemn fact bewailed by our legislators, even while they cling to the barbarous punishment.

Apparently, the efforts to save Mary's life were not supported by everyone in the town, for some Ministers of Religion and some women had refused to sign the petition to Sir George Grey, the Home Secretary.

They had rested their case on the Old Testament interpretation of the Scriptures which demanded 'an eye for an eye and a tooth for a tooth.' To them the sentence of the court was appropriate, reflecting the magnitude of the offence, and serving as a warning to other young girls finding themselves in a similar predicament to Mary Prout. They challenged those who took a contrary view to prove their case from a study of the Scriptures. The Editor in his response commented

> Hence those who have sought to prevent the extreme penalty of death being inflicted on that miserable prisoner in the Haverfordwest Gaol, have been by some of the teachers of religion, defied to produce from the Scriptures one single passage condemning capital punishment.

He disagreed with their views in the strongest of terms.

> The man who is continually quoting the text book of his religion to justify him in strangling the life out of his fellow man, must necessarily entertain most dishonouring (sic) views of nature and intent of that religion, and of the benevolent and beneficial God from whom it proceeded.

While these scriptural arguments were raging, Mary was left to count the hours and the days in her solitary cell. She was unaware that moves were afoot to obtain a reprieve and to seek a commutation of her sentence.

In fact, Mary's plight had gained the sympathy of many throughout the county. Within the space of a week, 1,120 names had been collected and submitted to the High Sheriff for transmission to Sir George Grey, 'Praying her Majesty to extend her royal pardon to Mary Prout (who was convicted last week for the murder of her Child.) to the extent of saving her life.' It was signed by many influential dignitaries, including the High Sheriff himself, the Sheriff's Chaplain, the Under Sheriff, several members of the Bar, Grand and Petty Jurors, Justices of the County, the Mayor, Aldermen and Councillors, Professional Gentlemen and other inhabitants of the County and Town. The local MP, Mr. Scourfield, had also called in person at the Home Office to convey the feelings of a substantial number of his electors that the execution should not take place. Clearly, these were not anxious to witness the grotesque spectacle of a public hanging, especially one involving a young and somewhat naïve woman, in spite of the gravity of her offence. With so many acting on her behalf, it was no surprise that the Home Office took a more lenient view than was customary in many other cases of infanticide. On 18 July, the Under Sheriff, J. Rogers Powell, received the following letter.

> Sir,
> I am to signify to you the Queen's commands that the execution of the sentence of death passed upon Mary Prout now in Pembroke County Gaol, be respited until futher signification of Her Majesty's pleasure.
> Your obedient servant,
>
> G.Grey

On the 19 July, he passed the letter to the Editor of the *Telegraph*,

> Sir,
> As the accompanying commutation, which we have today received from Secretary Sir George Grey, relative to Mary Prout, now in gaol under sentence of death for murder, cannot fail to give satisfaction to your readers, I shall be obliged by your insertion of it in your next paper.

The Editor who had campaigned so vigorously against the death penalty was more than pleased to do so. In his editorial, he expresses his satisfaction that 'the extreme penalty of death will not be inflicted – and Haverfordwest relieved from the dread and brutalizing spectacle.' But he also referred to those who had ardently desired that the full rigour of the law be applied in the case of Mary Prout and who would be disappointed by the reprieve.

> And yet, to our surprise, we find that there are some persons in Haverfordwest who deplore that Mary Prout is not to be strangled. There are women who regret that she is not to be hung like a dog . . . and her dying struggles witnessed by a jeering and remorseless mob.

According to W.D. Phillips, the gallows was almost completed before the reprieve came. He acknowledged the gravity of the crime committed by Mary, and accepted that it could not go unpunished. He did not desist from the view that her crime was murder and that it should be punished accordingly; his revulsion was to the death penalty.

> Let the wretched mother who murdered her own innocent child, live to repent her terrible sin, and seek the forgiveness of that merciful God who will pardon the vilest transgressor that is truly and sincerely repentant.

Mary was now sentenced to twenty years penal servitude, to be served in a London gaol, which would have been more than ample time for her to reflect upon her crime. In 1864, 1,730 infants under the age of one died in violent circumstances and many of these would be classed as infanticide. We shall never really know what took place in Mary's mind when she threw Rhoda into the Little Pit on that fateful day. We can only surmise that it was the result of the unbearable pressure placed upon her by a condemnatory society which regarded the birth of a child out of wedlock as a cardinal sin. With no one to turn to, she had been driven to commit one of the most heinous of crimes. Even today, questions relating to infanticide provoke a great deal of controversy, in spite of the fact that post-natal depression is now a recognised condition. In the case of Mary Prout, however, there was a happier conclusion. After serving ten years of her sentence, she was released from prison. She returned to Pembrokeshire, subsequently married a local man and had children. One mystery remains, however: who was Rhoda's father, and why indeed did Mary never reveal his name?

CHAPTER SIX

A WILLING MARTYR

'My heart is almost broken'

On Wednesday, 15 October,1740, a wan and forlorn figure stood near the old town hall in Hay-on-Wye with a Bible in his hand: he was attempting to preach the Gospel to a foul-mouthed barbaric mob. The crowd, far from accepting his offer of salvation, jeered and taunted him. Yet, he bravely persisted. He tried to sing and then attempted to pray, but his voice was drowned by a cacophony of offensive insults and loud heckling. The noise soon attracted many who were pillars of the community, including Justices of the Peace and even some gentlemen of the cloth. Far from being supportive and urging the mob to desist, these merely urged them on. They were infuriated by the fact that the lone preacher was seeking to convert people to the Methodist cause. Soon all kinds of obnoxious missiles were being directed at him; a trumpet was blown and someone started thumping a kettle drum; the Sexton started tolling the church bells in order to disrupt his sermon, and a fierce tragedy was about to unfold.

Today, Hay-on-Wye is a quaint, atmospheric border town lying in the shadow of the Black Mountains. It is widely renowned for its bookshops, where bibliophiles from far and wide can happily browse, hoping to chance upon a rare bargain. Once a year, in the month of May, it hosts a prestigious arts festival attracting illustrious names from the world of literature. Hay, then, becomes a byword for those who cherish culture, but on that sorry October day in 1740, the atmosphere was markedly different.

Badsey House – the family home of William Seward, occupied by his mother and elder brother, Henry.

The preacher was William Seward, an early adherent to the Methodist cause. Born in 1702 at Badsey near Evesham, he was the fifth son of John Seward, sometime steward to Lord Windsor who held estates in south Wales. Following a grammar-school education, William had carved for himself a successful career with the South Sea Company. So successful was he that the Earl of Egmont referred to him as 'the broker of Exchange Alley.' In 1732, Seward married, but throughout their brief marriage, his wife was a prey to all kinds of ailments. She died in 1736, leaving Seward to bring up their only child Gracey, who was named after her mother.

By this time, Seward had accumulated considerable wealth and was a man of some social standing. He could, like many of his contemporaries, have pursued a life of luxury, but within him there were deeper yearnings. Philanthropic by nature, he devoted much of his time and money to setting up charity schools and paid for an altar, a clock and new box pews for the church at Badsey. His charitable work brought him into contact with George Whitefield, a charismatic young preacher who was involved in a venture to establish an orphanage in Georgia for 'the children of slaves'. At this time Methodism, under the influence of John and Charles Wesley, was beginning to assail the foundations of the complacent Anglican orthodoxy: their powerful sermons attracted those who sought a deeper and more radical set of religious beliefs and Seward was ripe for such an experience. In his journal, he relates how he was converted by the evangelical zeal of Charles Wesley in November 1738:

> I cannot sufficiently praise God for bringing me out of that darkness into His marvellous light . . . This is a faith I never really felt before Mr. Charles Wesley expounded it to me. I cannot but always honour him as an instrument in God's hand for showing me the true way of salvation by Jesus Christ.

Although he never doubted Seward's convictions, Wesley appreciated that he could never make his mark as a fiery preacher. Even so, he was generous to a fault and offered to pay the cost of hiring a coach for him as he conducted services in the suburbs of London. Wesley declined the offer.

Bruised by the recent death of his wife, the powerful message conveyed by Wesley had enabled him to find 'peace with God'. In the same year, his father died and he succeeded him as the Steward of the Windsor Estates which included Cardiff Castle. George Whitefield was another fervent adherent to the Methodist cause and William Seward also invited him to preach at Badsey. Unfortunately, within his family there were ambivalent views: his brother Benjamin Seward, a prosperous businessman, had embraced Methodism, but his eldest brother Henry who still lived at Badsey, was much more sceptical. In spite of this, he received Whitefield with civility and allowed him to preach in his back yard because the church had been closed to him. The following day Whitefield again preached at Badsey, and so powerful was his message that he left a 'weeping audience'. Seward's youngest brother Thomas was an Anglican clergyman and he had no time at all for the Methodists. He was an affable but ineffectual cleric who became Canon of Lichfield and he was referred to by Horace Walpole as a 'pompous ass'. Also an aspiring poet, his work was derided and mocked by no less a figure than Dr Johnson. William Seward had long realised that he was a lost cause as far as Methodism was concerned.

In March 1739, Seward accompanied Whitefield on a crusading mission to Wales. In his journal he notes that

> We met our dear brother Howell Harris at Cardiff for the furtherance
> of the Gospel in Wales – where indeed it flourishes more than in
> England . . . Mr. Howell Harris goes from place to place and has been
> a mighty instrument of Reformation and of pulling down Satan's
> strongholds. O how my heart burns within me to hear him. He is a
> thundering preacher.

This first encounter with Howel Harris, the foremost Methodist
revivalist in Wales, had a profound effect on Seward and he was to
remain close to him for the remainder of his life. Methodism was an
unpopular and heretical cause in the eyes of many within the religious
establishment. Those who sought to promote it faced many
provocations and, on occasions, downright hostility. In Cardiff, while
Whitefield sought to preach to a crowd, a dead fox was thrown at his
feet and a pack of hounds let loose causing much confusion. Although
the early Methodists still regarded themselves as Anglicans, the Church
itself disavowed them and actively discouraged those who were
sympathetic to their cause. The local gentry often egged on mobs of
drunken hooligans who bellowed and roared to drown out their
sermons. Some even went further, ringing bells, blowing horns,
throwing eggs and all kinds of filth at the evangelists. Others armed
themselves with cudgels, staves and stones and were prepared to assault
them physically. Such was William Seward's admiration for Whitefield
and for Howel Harris that he was prepared to subject himself to all
manner of dangers. In fact, he seemed to revel in situations where
conflict was possible, although he could not match the doughty
presence of Whitfield and Howel Harris.

His support for Whitefield extended beyond the need to stand
alongside him when he sought converts to the cause. He willingly laid
aside his business interests and decided to support his friend's work in
Georgia. He wrote:

> I have settled my wordly affairs and have taken care of my dear child.
> God has begun a great work in our house.

In January 1739, they embarked for America in order to fulfil
Whitefield's dream of establishing an 'Orphan House' in the colony.

Seward had negotiated a substantial loan amounting to £8,000, taking £3,000 of it with him in cash. He used £2,000 to purchase 5,000 acres of land in Pennsylvania to establish a school for slaves and to set up a 'settlement for Methodists from England, where they might worship in their own way without being thought enthusiasts'. He also purchased a small ship to enable Whitefield to continue his evangelical work along the east coast of America. Seward's generosity was an important factor in promoting Whitefield's work in the New World, but it was to cause problems in years to come. They returned in March 1739 to continue evangelising in London. No place was beyond their reach. They even visited Bethlehem Hospital, or 'Bedlam', the horrendous asylum where, in an age where mental illness was not understood, so-called 'lunatics' were incarcerated in appalling conditions. There they discovered that Joseph Perian, a Methodist, had been confined for showing too much 'enthusiasm' and 'praying so loud, so as to be heard four storeys high . . . and that he sold his clothes and gave the money to the poor'. Seward, shocked by the treatment of this brother in the faith, persuaded the authorities to release him.

Whitefield continued to impress Seward as thousands flocked to hear him preach. As he was by now barred from preaching within recognised places of worship, he turned his attention to those who were deemed to be outside the pale of the established church. Seward noted that having been

> thrust out of the Synagogues, our brother has settled an exposition at Newgate (Prison) every morning . . . he has preached from 1500 to 15,000 hearers . . . once a week he preaches on the steps of a workhouse . . . he preaches among colliers – Thus the Gospel spreads around the country. – We are being set up for being stark mad . . . but the harvest is great.

Meanwhile, William Seward's obsession with Methodism was causing a split in the family at home. Henry Seward, the eldest brother, was becoming increasingly uneasy at William's deep involvement with the cause. An irritable, hot-tempered man, he became convinced that the Wesley brothers had turned his brother into an 'unbalanced bigot' and that they were only interested in the family wealth. When Charles Wesley

George Whitefield preaching.

visited his other brother Benjamin, he decided to act. As a magistrate he had a great deal of authority in the community and he had four constables posted outside his brother's house to prevent Wesley from gaining access. There developed a furious altercation between Charles Wesley and Henry Seward. Wesley was accused of causing a rift in the Seward family, but as Benjamin was ill and confined to bed, there was no one to defend the evangelist. Men were sent to duck Wesley in the river Avon, but mercifully he escaped. When he eventually managed to enter Benjamin Seward's house, there was more unpleasantness. An insanely irate Henry seized Charles Wesley by the nose, and only when Benjamin's wife called out did he release it, leaving a much shaken Charles Wesley.

Blissfully unaware of Wesley's difficulties with his brother Henry, William Seward returned to America in February 1740 in the company of Whitefield to 'fight Satan in the strongholds of Philadelphia'. Whitefield had now purchased land in Pennsylvania with the £2,000 provided by Seward. It was still his intention to build a school for the sons of slaves in order to 'save their souls' rather than to secure their freedom. Seward even argued in favour of slavery in Georgia, pointing

out that 'four slaves could be kept as cheaply as one white servant'.
Nevertheless, he was intent upon saving their souls.

> I visited a Negro and prayed with her and found her touched by divine
> grace. Praised be the Lord, methinks one Negro brought to Christ is
> particularly sweet to my soul. Oh! May the Lord make his power
> known among them too.

The voices of William Wilberforce and his fellow abolitionists had not
as yet been heard in England.

In April 1740, Seward decided to return to England and boarded
'The George' for the arduous journey home. Although somewhat timid
by nature, he had been inspired by Whitefield's missionary zeal and
spent much of his time and energy trying to convert his fellow
passengers and the sailors to the cause of Methodism. He did not meet
with a great deal of success and was ordered by the Captain to desist
from preaching because the sailors needed to concentrate on bringing
the ship safely to harbour. On 19 June he landed at Hastings and went
immediately to London in order to sell another £2,000 of his South Sea
Stock to finance Whitefield's work in Philadelphia.

On returning to Badsey in August, he became extremely concerned
about the spiritual welfare of his own mother who had not as yet
embraced the Methodist cause. Nevertheless, he asked for her blessing,
'and prayed and gave thanks for the great mercies God has shown me
since I was here last'. He was delighted to hear that the church bells were
to be rung to herald his return, but he might have been even more
appreciative if the hymns of Charles Wesley had been sung. To complete
his joy, his brother Benjamin came over from Bengeworth to greet him
and many of the Methodist converts from Evesham also turned up. When
the brothers expressed the wish to hold a meeting at 5am in Badsey
House, Henry Seward reluctantly agreed, but made it plain that he would
not attend. William continued to worry about his mother's salvation and
wrote, 'I was drawn to pray that she might see the Lord Christ before she
goes hence'. This infuriated Henry who had always been a dutiful son, a
conscientious church warden and, like his mother, a regular worshipper at
Badsey Church. By now William was so fanatical in his beliefs that he
regarded any outside the Methodist fold as being beyond redemption.

These included his own brother Henry, whom he now likened to a 'son of the devil' and one in a 'state of damnation'. Their bitter disagreements over doctrine continued and after three weeks William decided to leave Badsey stating, 'I told them I did not desire to leave the Church, and that I only desired to bring them to Jesus Christ'. William's religious convictions were now so strong that he could no longer brook any dissenting views. They outweighed any affection or loyalty that he felt towards members of his own family, and they were never again to see him alive. On 26 August he left for Wales having failed to 'save' his mother, but he was still full of hope that he would fulfil his destiny in the company of the mighty Welsh revivalist Howel Harris.

He called first at Cheltenham and was dismayed at the worldly prosperity of the place. People came there to drink the waters for the relief of bodily ailments, but they were totally oblivious to the need to cleanse their souls. He exhorted them not to partake of sinful activities; otherwise the waters would become waters of affliction and not of healing. But his pleas, as usual, fell on deaf ears. The gentry and their ladies who ostensibly swarmed to these spa towns for the sake of their health came also to gamble, to eat and drink, and to be seen in fashionable society. The sight of Seward as some latter-day John the Baptist emerging from the desert uttering dire warnings about hellfire were met with derision rather than awe. On 3 September he had reached Abergavenny, where he was joined by Howel Harris, now the established leader of Welsh Methodism. Seward began to preach in the open air, a severe test, bearing in mind the general hostility which still prevailed in society at large. But his first attempt filled him with exultation as he observed that he

> was assisted to speak to them with power – Glory to God alone – this was the first time I spoke in the air, and the awfulness of the mountains and hills drawed (sic) me to consider the Majesty of Him who setteth fast the mountains and is girded about with power.

The beauty of his Welsh surroundings had proved to be an inspiration.

On 6 September they reached Caerphilly, 'where Brother Harris discoursed on a mountain in Welsh'. Both of them then sang, prayed and exhorted the crowd not to rest in anything 'less than in the full assurance of faith'. His next visit to Cardiff proved to be more peaceful than his first, for 'never did the people show so great a readiness to hear sermons . . . Religion has become the subject of most conversation'. In Cowbridge he reminded the listeners that two years previously he had come to the town as Steward of the Lord of the Manor, but that he had now come as Steward to the Lord of Lords. He told them that he had turned his back on material things to follow his conscience.

> I might have kept my footman and brace of geldings and gone to Bath and Tunbridge in the manner gentlemen do . . . but the happiness of a man's life does not consist of the abundance of things we possess, but in righteousness, peace, joy . . . and the Holy Ghost.

Sensitive to the fact that the vast majority of his Welsh audiences were unfamiliar with the English language, he suggested that a printing press be set up at Pontypool to promote the Gospel through the Welsh language and also that a school be established at Harris's home in Trefeca to train aspirants for the ministry.

The comparative calm of his Welsh visit was soon to be broken, for 9 September was not destined to be a peaceful day.

> Rose early . . . we went to Newport where Satan was permitted to rage against us for about 2 hours . . . We went to discourse in the market place . . . the mob began to pelt us like persons in the pillory . . . Brother Harris received a little hurt on his forehead where blood appeared.

This experience did nothing to dissuade Seward, for he felt that the power of God enabled him to 'withstand the insults of the mob' so that he was able to return blessings for curses. For half an hour they had a quiet discourse – then a certain person 'raved like a madman and cursing and swearing strove to pull them down'. There was now much scuffling and Seward described how he was 'pushed off the table which we had removed to the middle of the market place but got upon it again. We were much moved to pity and pray for them'. The crowd continued to taunt them with 'oaths, blasphemy, whoredoms, adulteries and profanation of the Lord's Day and Harris had his coat sleeve pulled off'. Later that night they reached Caerleon. At first the situation seemed reasonably calm, but after they had prayed and sung for about half an hour, an unruly mob gathered. The reception was even worse than that encountered in Newport. Rotten eggs, dung and even a dead cat were thrown at them. The town fire engine was brought out to drench them and a large drum beaten to drown out their preaching. Seward recorded the experience in his journal,

> The noise drowned our voices till at length I was struck with a stone, brickbat, or some other hard substance upon my right eye which caused so much anguish that I was forced to go away to the Inn and put an end to my discourse. It was given to me to pray all the way for the poor people and especially for the person who struck me. Brother Harris continued to discourse for some time after & the other brethren declared their testimony against them.

Seward had intended to go on that night to Pontypool, but the condition of his eye demanded immediate attention. After he had it attended to he went to bed and the following morning he wrote, 'Blessed be God, I slept in the arms of my dear Jesus'. In the meantime, a resilient Howel Harris was minded to preach again at Caerleon. Seward was in no condition to assist him, but in spite of the entreaties of friends he was determined to accompany his mentor.

> I was led by the hand because of the dressing on my eyes . . . persons that knew my father came kindly to entreat us to come away from the mob, but the Lord gave me freedom to stay till Brother Harris had fully delivered his testimony. We had discharged our consciences.

Their next venue was Usk and after an early start they reached it at mid-afternoon. One of the brethren had to lead Seward's horse as the pain was so intense in his right eye that his vision was impaired. They received a warmer welcome here and were allowed to make use of the Town Hall. Seward was mightily relieved that their work could continue without the usual threat from a hostile mob and he recorded his gratitude in his journal.

> I never had greater assistance nor ever spoke to so large an audience
> . . . Howel Harris repeated the address in Welsh . . . And all bore
> record that we were sent from God.

On 11 September, 1740, they set out again for Monmouth, with
Seward still partially blind having to be led by the hand. Unbeknown to
them this was the day of the races, and assembled in the town was the
Duke of Beaufort accompanied by a large number of the local gentry
and their ladies. In spite of his infirmity, Seward bravely decided to
address the crowd.

> We discoursed to great numbers . . . some of the baser sort being
> drunk attempted to pull us down but the Jailer hindered them. When I
> was speaking the Bailiff came to read the Act of Parliament . . . We
> set a table before us into the Market Place over against the Town Hall
> where the gentry and the nobles were met for dinner. We both got
> upon the table and I began to sing after Brother Harris exhorted with
> great power near an hour.

Unfortunately, they had both misconstrued the temper of their audience.
The majority were there for the races and were in no mood to listen to the
exhortations of the two evangelists. Their mood soon turned ugly as
Seward and Harris were subjected to 'continual showers of stones, plums,
walnuts, dirt and also a dead dog'. Seward was again struck on his
forehead and under his right eye by stones 'But blessed be to God, neither
of us had any great hurt'. They continued to sing, but as usual a drum was
beaten to drown out their voices. Sheltered by their evangelical zeal they
refused to be intimidated, 'although Satan raged against us'. Eventually,
however, Howel Harris had to lead his companion away by the hand as he
was hardly able to see and was completely disorientated. It is not
surprising that their reception at Monmouth was so hostile as it appears
that in his sermon Harris had delivered a diatribe against the sins of
dancing and horse racing. He also told the assembled mob that 'their sins
did draw a curse upon the nation'. Many of the gentry had known
Seward's father in his capacity as Steward to the Duke of Beaufort, and
some of them urged him to go home out of harm's way. They received an
icy response, as Seward noted,

They pitied me, but I entreated them to pity their own souls and ways for themselves and their own children.

The wanderings of the two revivalists were to continue, but even Seward's unquestionable fervour was to be tested when on 12 September, 1740, Howel Harris suggested that they should return to Monmouth. He confessed that 'my flesh began to rebel and a slavish fear came upon me'. After his previous experiences, who can blame him? Even so, he decided to 'throw himself at Jesus' feet' and to await a response. The message was to 'Follow Brother Harris'. Nevertheless, he continued to harbour many doubts and fears. In particular, he feared for his eyesight as Harris had to lead his horse, and he confessed that he rode, 'as a thief to the gallows or a bear to the stake or as a lamb to the slaughter'. They both knew that they were risking their lives, but their commitment to their cause overcame any concern for their own physical well-being. News of their coming was 'soon noised abroad, and the Engine and Drum was set in the Market Place'. They had been warned that should they attempt to speak they would be killed. Fortunately, after much prayer, they decided to heed the warning and instead of going to Monmouth they went to Coleford, Mitcheldean and Gloucester.

Meanwhile, the Wesley brothers were also campaigning in Wales. John visited the country on thirty-five occasions mainly to support Howel Harris. There was also a Welsh connection since Charles had married Sarah Gwyn of Garth, the daughter of a prominent Methodist family in Breconshire. The brothers were also frequently attacked, and John, like Harris and Seward, was roughly treated during a visit to Cowbridge. 'The sons of Belial gathered together, cursing, blaspheming and throwing stones without intermission . . . I judged it best to dismiss the congregation.' Undeterred, he ventured into the remotest part of Cardiganshire, and in attempting to reach Ffair Rhos, he found himself 'wandering through rough bogs and precipices'. Eventually, he came to a tavern 'full of drunken, roaring miners' who worked in the local lead mines. He hired one of them to show him the way, but by this time his mare was bleeding from a wound so progress was slow. Nevertheless, the influence of Daniel Rowland of Llangeitho had pervaded mid

Cardiganshire, and when he eventually reached Tregaron and then Lampeter, much to his delight the 'congregations overflowed'.

Howel Harris now decided to part company with Seward and to return to Wales. Before doing so, he was invited to read Seward's journal and he concluded that it was 'strong meal and simple'. He urged its publication, and Seward agreed to remedy those aspects of 'its great plainness and simplicity' which Harris had noted as its only weakness. Without the companionship of his Welsh mentor, Seward now made his way to Upton-on-Severn and came upon a Methodist feast. His cordial reception was in stark contrast to his unfortunate experiences in Wales. He provides a vivid description of the scene.

> Several brethren and sisters came from Gloucester and we spent about 6 hours in singing, prayer and exhortation, having a love feast of bread and cheese and water, and dear souls were fed with the Bread of Life and the Waters of Comfort till we could hold no more. – The Master of the Feast was indeed with us and sat in the midst of us – we felt His presence in our hearts as really as the disciples saw Him with their own eyes at the Last Supper.

Seward continued his ministry in Gloucestershire where he found the congregations friendly and responsive. On occasions, however, he is assailed by self doubt and a feeling that he is unworthy to proclaim the message. In his journal he refers to himself as 'a poor nothing worm' and adds 'O may I abhor myself in dust and ashes'. In spite of these moments, he continued with his mission and at Stroud his confidence was boosted by his reception on 13 September, 1740.

> Many Justices, it being the Quarter Sessions. I was drawn to press the rich to come to Jesus. I was helped to tell them that if I had been so minded, I might have indulged as much as any Gent. in England – in all sorts of fashionable diversions, but that the Grace of God had snatched me out of the burning, and therefore I was constrained to seek the salvation of others . . . there were very few scoffers.

Seward felt elated, but his joy was not to last.

The following day, although clearly unwell and totally exhausted, he forced himself to continue preaching.

Went into the street, enabled to speak for nearly 2 hours . . . finding my frail nature wanted sleep, I lay before the fire and slept sweetly in the arms of my Dear Jesus.

Unfortunately, at national level, a rift was developing between the Wesleys and Whitefield. The primary cause of the dissension was Whitefield's belief in 'double predestination'. The Wesleys regarded this as an erroneous doctrine and insisted that the love of God was universal. Seward had a close affinity with Whitefield and tended to subscribe to his views. Nevertheless, he travelled to Bristol where he was met by the Wesley brothers but he was extremely upset when they refused to allow him to speak to the Society. He was also distressed on learning that the Wesleys did not approve of his precious journal because it 'bore explicit testimony to the doctrine of Election' which they rejected. It also became evident that they did not have a very high opinion of his abilities as a preacher. Hurt by these criticisms, Seward responded by telling Charles Wesley that although he had been converted by him, he now regarded him as a 'minister of Satan'. He poured a torrent of invective into his Journal, calling the brothers 'Judases and wolves in sheep's clothing'. The Wesleys were embarrassed by this open display of hostility from one who had in the past so generously supported their cause. They feared that so public a disagreement was harming Methodism and they sought a reconciliation. Seward was not easily placated, and continued to rage against his former friends in his journal.

> The Lord made a means of opening my eyes to see that Satan has deceived Brother Wesley by turning himself into an Angel of Light. They both rejected my Journal and Mr. Charles Wesley slighted all the great things which my dear Jesus has lately done by my weak hands.

There were further efforts to heal the rift but Seward refused to compromise. The affair was having an effect on his health, which was never robust, and a friend suggested that he was in need of a doctor. In his journal he continually fulminates against Charles Wesley in particular, and maintains that God has drawn him towards Whitefield in this dispute.

> The Lord drew me to follow Mr. Whitefield and not Mr. Wesley . . .
> Now I see through grace that a man may give all his goods to the poor
> and his body to be burnt and yet have no Charity . . . Satan has
> deceived Brother Wesley for he knew not what he did . . . It was with
> much sorrow and heaviness of heart – but I could no longer have
> fellowship with Brother Wesley.

There was another attempt on the part of the Wesleys to reach an accord
when Seward was invited by Charles Wesley and some friends to a
meeting on 25 September, 1740. He records in his journal that Wesley
'wanted to reconcile matters and to labour for peace'. Their efforts
were unsuccessful, and the journal now reflects a perverse and
uncompromising side to Seward's character.

> It was given to me to answer that there was no peace. I was also
> moved to deal plainly with his soul and say, Thou child of the Devil,
> Enemy of all righteousness, Bond of iniquity – whereupon he decreed
> that we might pray, which at first I declined, but after complied.

Charles Wesley was dismayed at the pejorative remarks in Seward's
journal which could only serve to widen the rift between the Wesleys
and Whitefield. He communicated this concern to George Whitefield in
the hope that he could in some way influence his friend.

> The well meaning Mr. Seward has caused the world to triumph in our
> supposed dissension, by his unseasonable journal. Your zealous
> indiscreet friends, instead of concealing any little difference between
> us have told it in Gath.

There was to be no reconciliation, but, by his own admission, the whole
affair continued to torment Seward: 'These trials caused me great
oppression – my soul is exceeding sorrowful.' What is more, 'My body
is weak and my strength somewhat failing.' This might have been due
to the fact that he had been following an extremely frugal diet, which he
now decided to abandon.

> I have lived on vegetables and water for several months, but this
> day[September27] I ate a little meat and drank some wine for my
> stomach's sake – and blessed be God I was strengthened.

The Wesleys still persevered, and on 30 September Charles again met Seward and invited him to pray with him. Yet again, he was rebuffed. In an attempt to escape from what had become a very acrimonious situation, Seward turned once again towards Wales. He had heard that Howel Harris had been attacked in Hereford and he continued to express his great admiration for his erstwhile companion in the faith. He arranged to meet him on 11 October at Erwood.

> Br. Harris met me at 4 o' clock . . . We sat up singing and praying till 5 in the morning . . . and on our return home our hearts were much affected. We fell on each other's necks and prayed till 3 in the morning and felt great love and unity.

On 12 October we find Seward at Trefeca where again he and Harris sat up late discussing doctrine. Harris did not see the need to oppose the Wesley brothers and managed to mollify Seward's anger to some extent. After this conversation he was persuaded to declare, 'O may we be one in the Lord Jesus'.

He now embarked on a relentless campaign; on Monday 13 October he spoke on the Beatitudes to about 1,000 people in Brecon. That night he returned to Trefeca to continue the discussion on doctrine until 3am, and once again he and Harris felt 'great love and unity'. Two days later after an 'affectionate parting' he set out for Hay-on-Wye after agreeing to meet again at Abergavenny 'by the will of God'. But it was not to be.

He started preaching outside the castle in Hay, and although he was accompanied by a few supporters, a number of people urged on by the local worthies turned against him, and he soon became the usual target for their missiles of dirt, dung, stones and rotten eggs. Church bells were clanged and he was subjected to torrents of foul-mouthed abuse. Fragile and debilitated, Seward was in no condition to withstand the raw hostility of the mob, egged on by those purporting to be pillars of society. During his brief ministry he had been spat upon and grievously assaulted on many occasions, but he always found the strength to pray for the souls of his persecutors. This time, however, a large stone was hurled hitting him on the back of his head causing serious injury. He was carried away by his friends to a place of safety. That night, although in great discomfort, he was able to write these lines in his journal.

> Wednesday, 15, October, came to Hay and attempted to discourse a little from the town; but after singing a prayer and discoursing for a few minutes, the Minister of the Parish and several Justices of the Peace, with many other Clergymen came and demanded my silence and stirred up the people against (me).

Over the next few days his condition deteriorated and he died on 22 October, 1740, a week after addressing the hostile crowd at Hay. In spite of his pain he prayed for the person who had cast the stone and asked that no action be taken against him. When the news of his death reached Howel Harris, he was devastated and filled with grief,

> Heard that my dear Bro. Seward is gone to Heaven . . . Recollecting Bro. Seward's work and simplicity and especially his being buffeted with me with dung . . . it was more than I could bear, my heart is almost broken.

The late Reverend Peter Braby, Vicar of Badsey, noted in the diary of the Earl of Egmont the following contemporary reference to Seward's death:

> Mr. Seward lost his life in Glostershire (sic) by a stone cast at him while preaching in the fields.

The Wesley brothers also expressed their deep sorrow at his death. John wrote on 27 October, 1740,

> The surprising news of poor Mr. Seward's death was confirmed. Surely, God will maintain His own cause. Righteous are Thou, O Lord.

Charles expressed similar sentiments.

> I was exceedingly shocked with the news of Mr. Seward's death; but he is taken from evil; rescued out of the hands of wicked men.

A letter from Henry Newman, Secretary of the Society for the Promotion of Christian Knowledge, dated 11 November, 1740 also refers to the circumstances surrounding William Seward's death.

> It has been rumoured that Mr. Seward met with some insult which drew upon him a fever which hastened his end.

As for Whitefield, the loss of his friend and patron was a cruel blow. All his plans for an orphanage in Savannah came to nought; even worse, he was imprisoned for debt in Philadelphia. The large sum of money promised by Seward for the school for slaves, and for which he had stood as guarantor, had not been paid. His untimely death meant that no provision had been made for Whitefield's grand designs and he alone became responsible for the debts so far incurred. William Seward was buried in the churchyard at Cusop, two miles from Hay and across the border into Herefordshire. The following inscription was carved on his grave, but the year of his death is incorrect.

> Here lyeth the body of William Seward of Badsey in the County of Worcester Gent. Who departed ye life October ye 22 1742 (sic) Aged 38.

The plaque inside the church refers to his devotion:

> To the cause of Christ in the Great Evangelical Revivals in England, Wales and America.', and goes on to say that he was 'A friend and supporter of John and Charles Wesley, George Whitefield and Howel Harris of Trefeca.

The plaque also records the circumstances of his death.

> He was injured on a preaching tour in South Wales in the autumn of 1740 and died a week after he had spoken to hostile crowds in Hay.

Throughout his short life William Seward had lived in the shadow of two of the most powerful figures of the Methodist Revival, George Whitefield and Howel Harris. It was claimed that Harris had a voice

Howel Harris.

In Memory
of
WILLIAM SEWARD
BORN BADSEY WORCESTERSHIRE 1702
HE DEVOTED HIMSELF TO THE CAUSE OF CHRIST IN THE GREAT EVANGELICAL REVIVALS
IN ENGLAND, WALES, AND AMERICA.
HE WAS A FRIEND AND SUPPORTER OF JOHN AND CHARLES WESLEY, GEORGE WHITEFIELD
AND HOWEL HARRIS OF TREFECA.
HE WAS INJURED ON A PREACHING TOUR IN SOUTH WALES IN THE AUTUMN OF 1740
AND DIED A WEEK AFTER HE HAD SPOKEN TO HOSTILE CROWDS IN HAY.
HE IS BURIED IN THIS CHURCHYARD.
"FOR ME TO LIVE IS CHRIST AND TO DIE IS GAIN."
"CANYS BYW I MI YW CRIST A MARW SYDD ELW."

Plaque in Cusop Church.

like a gale with the power to transfix congregations, and although the gentry had hunted them 'like partridges', he had always sought to protect his loyal companion. But Seward was always conscious of the fact that he did not possess the eloquence and the physical stamina of these two revivalists.

> Mr. Howel Harris has been a means under God – he goes from place to place preaching and exhorting, he has been a means of pulling down Satan's strongholds, revelry, swearing, gambling, cockfighting and ye like. Oh how my heart burns within me to hear him and our dear Bro. Whitfield tell of their experiences. Would that I had the strength to follow them.

Seward is now regarded as the first Methodist martyr. The stone cast at Hay may have led to his death, but the numerous assaults he had endured over the previous two years while delivering his message had weakened him and greatly impaired his health. There can be no doubt that he gave his life for a cause he so fervently believed in and, on occasions, so fanatically espoused. One of the last entries in his journal is a prayer requesting that he be released from the travails of this world in order to gain the reward that he had so fervently prayed for during his short life:

> Oh that I may lay down my head and fall asleep in the arms of my Lord.